A Father's Choice

A Father's Choice

Shalynn Mellerup

Illustrated by Delvin Mellerup

CONTENTS

CONTENTS

To true love... and all the work that
goes into it.

Prologue

The king made his way through the palace. Affairs of state would never wait on a man, not even a king. His son rushed up from behind him.

"Father! Father! Come and see what I've found!" Tristan said.

He tugged at the king's hand, drawing him towards a new discovery. The king laid a hand on the boy's head, halting him. He looked up with his mother's eyes and grinned.

The king's heart stuttered. It was a wonder it had not stopped altogether from the grief of losing his queen. Now here was this child of theirs growing up so quickly.

But there were meetings to attend to, diplomats

to soothe, and political problems to solve. There was no time to cater to a growing boy's dreams.

"I'm sorry, Tristan. Another time."

The king left his son standing in the hallway. It was not the first time... And most certainly, it was not the last.

Chapter 1

The years crept by, adding lines to the king's face and silver to his hair. His love for his kingdom and his son grew, but time... there was only so much time and so many people depended on his leadership. It was much too easy to leave his son in the capable hands of his tutors. Much too easy to let time pass by.

By the time the king finally saw the gift he had allowed to slip through his fingers, the chasm was deep. Messages went unreturned, invitations to spend time together were refused, requests to meet were disregarded. His vibrant son had grown into a cynical young man with the world at his fingertips.

On the anniversary of his wife's death, the king pondered the matter in his rooms. Affairs of state *would* wait. He had learned his lesson too late, but he had learned it.

He looked in the mirror. Age had settled on his shoulders. How long would it be before he was no longer able to rule his people? What kind of a ruler would he leave them in his son?

He glanced up at the portrait of his wife.

"I wish you were here," he murmured, "What should I do with this son of ours? I'm so sorry. I haven't done right by him. I haven't raised him the way you would have wanted."

He paused, "How do I help him now? He won't talk to me, he won't listen."

The king sighed and wandered out onto his balcony. He had been a young man once, impulsive and rash. And then he met a princess...

The king smiled. She had changed him. His wife had made him a better man, a better ruler.

A wife... the king mulled the idea over. Of course, Tristan would marry eventually but would

it be wrong to encourage the process? Or even...
seek the kind of bride his son needed?

The king frowned. The idea had merit but his
son would never accept his guidance on the choice
of a bride. They had lost that closeness long ago.

He could choose a bride for his son. Tristan
would hate him. Tristan already hated him. In that
respect, the king fully suspected he had nothing
to lose.

He straightened, grimly surveying the kingdom
before him, the kingdom he would pass on to his
son. That was it then. He would comb the kingdom for a worthy bride. For his son's sake. For the
sake of his kingdom's future.

There were only two questions left... First, who
was the girl?

And second... would Tristan accept his father's
choice?

The king, feeling his age and more, looked out
over the daughters of his noblemen. After weeks of
traveling, he was tired. Every place he came to was

the same. They brought their daughters, adorned in silk and jewels. They paraded before him and their fathers argued their best attributes between themselves and to him. He was tired of listening.

Surely his son's bride was somewhere among them. He was just overlooking her somehow. He squinted at the young ladies before them as though it would allow him to see them in a new way. But all he could see was shallow smiles and vain posturing.

This wasn't what he wanted for his son. He wasn't looking for a great beauty. He wasn't looking for someone who was adept in social graces. He was looking for... something more. Something that he wasn't finding.

With a tight smile to one of his men, the king excused himself from the men who were yet trying to gain his attention for their daughters. The hallway was quiet. Then voices from the direction of the entrance made him turn and take the nearest door.

The steep, narrow stairs led him to the kitchen. The servants' chatter came to a halt as they realized who had stumbled into their domain. Spying a door on the far side, the king gave himself a royal decree to get some fresh air.

But as he pulled the door open, a blast of cold air hit him in the face. It was too cold to go out without a cloak or covering. His own was in his rooms but an old black coat hung by the door.

He turned back to the inhabitants of the kitchen, "Whose coat is this?"

A tall man toward the back of the room stepped forward, "Mine, your Majesty."

The king pulled the pouch of coins that he always carried from his belt. He pulled out two.

"May I prevail upon you to lend it to me?"

The two coins were more than enough to cover the cost of the coat. The oddness of the request was enough to make the man hesitate, but he knew his duty. He bowed low.

"Of course, your Majesty."

The king strode forward and pressed the coins

SHALYNN MELLERUP
Brook
Inn

into his hands with a smile of thanks. Then he strode from the kitchen and into the dying light of the day. It would take a miracle to make him feel young again.

~*~*~*~

A few hours later, an old man entered an inn. The door blew shut behind him. The inn was empty. The only other occupant of the room was a serving girl wiping the tables. The old man lowered himself into the chair nearest to the fire looking like the weight of the world rested on his shoulders... looking like the weight might shatter his heart.

The girl hesitated when she saw him. Then she finished wiping the table and disappeared into the kitchen. A moment later she reappeared with a tray with a clay pitcher and two mugs. She set the tray down and sat down at the table across from him.

"Hot cider," she said, "have some if you like."

He looked up with sad eyes.

"I'll be paying for it later, I suspect," he said, a bitter catch in his rich tone.

"No sir, dinner is closed. You won't be payin' a thing."

She pushed a full mug his way, "here."

He took it. They sat in silence, watching the flames.

"Is it... always this quiet here?" he asked a few minutes later.

"Sometimes," she said, "not always. I knew it would be tonight. Most of the people who come here are in the next town. They wanted to see the king."

The old man sighed, "I know."

The flames crackled in the silence. Then the girl spoke again.

"When I was younger, I asked my mother what made a king so special. She told me his heart is what makes a king special, that without a good heart, no man was really a king. Then she said that my father had the heart of a king because he loved us. I never cared, after that whether or not I ever saw... royalty."

Once again, flames were the only sound. They sipped the hot cider silently.

"Why?" said the old man.

"Because," she said, "Mama was right. Daddy was a real king. He...he was special. He set an example for my brothers to be kings among men."

"And you? What did he teach you?"

"Me?" she asked, "He taught me... to whistle. He taught me to be respectful to those around me. He taught me to look past appearances and not be hasty to judge. He taught me to watch for danger but not to be afraid. He taught me a lot."

"I didn't know..." the old man sighed, "I was never taught to be a good father. I'm afraid I'm learning far too late."

"How will you know if it's too late or not unless you try?" she asked quietly.

The old man smiled slightly, "Trying to be the voice of reason, are you?"

She laughed, "I'm sorry sir, I can't seem to help it. I have too many siblings to practice on, I guess."

"I see. And what is your name daughter-of-a-king?"

"Jenna," she answered, "my name is Jenna Longfellow."

The conversation continued late into the night. They talked about the weather, the state of the kingdom, their beliefs. Jenna stirred the fire and added wood. Jenna told him about her family; her six younger siblings and her mother. She told him about the day her father died. He told her about his late wife and how much he still missed her. He told her about watching his son grow up... How he realized how much of his son's childhood he had failed to be there for. How he knew that was a mistake now. They talked until the old man fell asleep.

The next morning, as the sun crept through the windows of the inn, the old man opened his eyes. A worn wool blanket was tucked around him. Sunlight made the room glow and all was silent. The old man sat up, not feeling so old anymore.

For the first time in years, he had slept peacefully. He stood feeling stronger. He set the blanket on the table. The world looked much brighter this morning... brighter than it had looked for many, many mornings.

Hoofbeats outside made him turn his head towards the door. One of his men rushed through.

"You're Highness!"

The man turned to a man behind him, "Send a messenger. He's here and he's well."

The man turned back to the old man, the king, "Are you alright, Sir?"

"I'm quite alright, Stevens. I haven't felt so well in ages," said the king.

"The men have been looking for you, Sir," said Stevens, "When we discovered you were missing this morning, the whole town was in an uproar. I tried to calm it but..."

"Hmm, I didn't mean to be gone so late."

"Sir," said Stevens, "respectfully, that was more than late."

"True," said the king, "Round up the innkeeper. It's time for breakfast."

The innkeeper, unaware that he had guests, had been eating his own breakfast in his own house which was connected to the inn. The sound of the horses, however, had brought him from his house to his yard, where Stevens found him. Soon breakfast was laid for the king and his men.

As they finished the meal, the king turned to Stevens.

"When I came here last night, there was a girl."

"A girl?"

"Yes, a girl. Her name is Jenna Longfellow. I want her found. I need to thank her."

"Yes, Sir."

Chapter 2

The sound of hoofbeats filled the air outside the Longfellow cottage. Jenna looked over her shoulder and finished hanging her piece of laundry. The little girl who was helping her ran inside. Jenna turned around to wait.

The horses stopped. The king was in front. He looked down from his horse. Curiosity flashed across Jenna's face, then was gone in a warm, gentle smile.

"Hello, Jenna."

"Hello, Sir."

The man on the next horse frowned and started

to speak. The king hushed him and ordered the men to fall back. When they did, he spoke to Jenna quietly.

"You took the time last night to talk to an old man. I thank you."

Jenna smiled, "It was nothing."

"It was everything," said the king, "Sometimes an old man forgets how to hope. If there's anything I can do to repay you..."

Jenna shook her head, "Thank you, Sir, but that's... that's not...that's not why I did it."

The king was still for an instant. Then he nodded, "I know."

He pulled out a bag of coins, "Will you take these anyway?"

Jenna was distressed, "Sir, I..."

"Please?" he asked.

Slowly Jenna nod-
ded. He handed her the
bag. Then he nodded
farewell and turned his
horse to go. Then he
turned it back to her.

He smiled almost

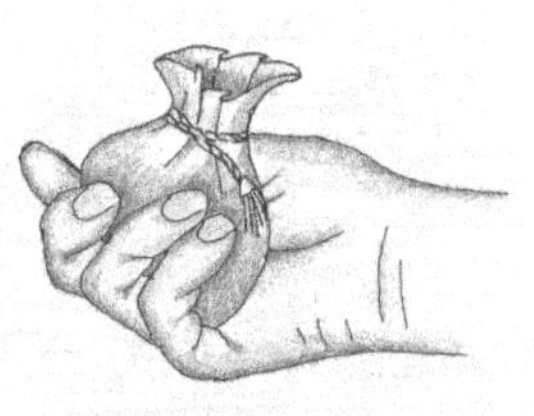

sheepishly, "Would you marry my son if I asked?"

Jenna laughed outright and in shock.

"No, Sir!"

He kind of chuckled, "I didn't think so."

~*~*~*

By the end of the month, Jenna's sixteen-year-old sister, Alana had a new dress. Her fifteen-year-old brother, Brandon, had a new axe; her thirteen-year-old brother, Timothy, had a new schoolbook.

Her next sister, Alexa, age twelve, had her own set of needles; and the youngest two, her brother seven and her sister six, had a wooden whistle and bead bracelet, respectively. For her mother she had bought material and together they sewed new curtains for their old cottage. The rest of the money they put away for later.

Jenna still worked at the inn. Her mother still took in sewing. But for the first time since their father died, her brothers were able to attend school. Her mother could afford oil for a lamp. They had enough.

Then the king returned.

He came to the inn while she was working. They all came, him and his men. They filled the inn, it seemed. Jenna looked up from where she was working just as the king saw her. His face was set and determined.

"Sir?" she asked.

"Jenna." He said, "You said you would not. But, Jenna, for your king, and for your country I'm begging you to change your mind."

Jenna swallowed hard. Confused expressions covered the faces of most of the soldiers, a few frowned. The customers, there to eat lunch, were as still as if they'd been carved from stone.

"Don't..." Jenna choked out, "I can't guess...what you're asking. I don't..."

Her voice choked off and she was unable to continue.

"You know," he said, "Jenna, I wouldn't ask if I saw another way."

Jenna's knuckles were turning white where she gripped the table. She said nothing.

The king sighed deeply.

"Jenna... I'm asking you to marry my son."

Jenna crumpled to the floor.

Chapter 3

A horrible smell pulled Jenna out of her faint. She gasped. She coughed.

When she opened her eyes, the room was empty except for the king, two soldiers, and the innkeeper with his wife's smelling salts. As she recalled the question, she felt the room start to spin again. *This is ridiculous,* she thought, *I don't faint.*

The innkeeper chuckled. Then he hushed as though worried the king might take offense. Jenna realized she had thought out loud. She let the king help her up onto a chair.

She rested her head on her hands. This was impossible. The problem was, it was so impossible that she knew she wasn't dreaming.

She looked up. They all expected her to say something.

"I don't know what to say..."

She tried to stand and felt the world tilt again. The innkeeper started to help her then shrank back nervously... which made *her* more nervous. The king took her arm to steady her.

"Maybe you should sit down," he suggested softly.

"I'm fine," she said, "I'll feel better to stand..."

The king turned to the innkeeper, "You. Fetch my men some ale."

He turned to the two soldiers and gestured to a table at the far end of the room, "You can wait over there."

Then he turned back to Jenna, "Sit down, Jenna."

Jenna stared at him blankly.

"Please, Jenna?" he said.

She slowly lowered herself into a chair. The king pulled another chair over and sat down.

"I know what I'm asking isn't easy, but we need you, Jenna."

Jenna shook her head slowly.

"We?" she asked, "and why?"

"The kingdom needs you. The people need

you. Maybe my son needs you. Maybe all he needs is someone to see him as a person instead of a prince. I don't know. But I do know that you have a way of looking past what a person is to see *who* they are. Jenna, I don't know what will happen if you come back to the palace with us... but if you don't I have no hope for this kingdom."

Jenna looked up at him, "You can see your son as more than a prince."

The king's face was gloomy, "I've ignored him too long for him to trust me. When he looks at me he sees a king not a father. When I look at him... I worry for my kingdom when I'm gone."

"If I go back with you," said Jenna, "he will probably hate me."

The king considered this, "He might."

"The nobility will be angry."

The king nodded slowly, "Yes."

"I could not place my family in the middle of that. I won't abandon them."

"They would be free to visit whenever they wished, as would you."

"It's not possible. It couldn't work."

"Jenna..."

"Sir, I'm only common. No one but you would ever accept me as... as the prince's wife."

"Jenna. I'm the king. I'm the only one who decides who is accepted; the rest would be of no concern."

"I beg your pardon, Sir, but that's not true. You can't lead those who won't follow."

The king sighed, "Your wisdom is beyond your years."

They sat still, in the heavy silence. At the far table, the two soldiers sipped their ale quietly. They dutifully ignored the king and his guest.

Finally, the king spoke.

"We could bring you in quietly. I could engage an etiquette instructor and hire a dressmaker. If they keep their silence, no one need know your common roots."

Jenna shook her head and frowned, almost angrily, "It wouldn't stay hidden long. Besides, I'm not ashamed of who I am or of my family."

The king was contrite. "I'm sorry, child. I was wrong to suggest such."

He was quiet for a moment before he continued.

"Yes, I was wrong. But I am not wrong about

who this kingdom needs," he leaned forward, "You are strong, diplomatic, you were patient with an old man, you have understanding and wisdom beyond your years... and you are the daughter of a king. A better king than I."

Jenna could almost see the painful memories of the king dancing across his face. Her heart ached with the choice to be made. She closed her eyes. The king watched as a tear rolled down her face.

"Jenna," he said, brokenly, quietly, "I leave this now as your choice. It must be your choice. Not mine."

Jenna sat still as, teardrop by teardrop, she made her choice. She had to try.

"Ok," she whispered, "Ok."

Jenna did not go home to tell her mother until she was more composed. Then she went alone. She walked home. The path that she walked every day seemed far too short. Soon she would reach home. Soon she would have to put the decision she had made into words. She couldn't even bring herself to think of it.

But the walk would go by quickly. She calmed herself. She thought.

How was it even possible? What would it mean to marry a prince? How many millions of little ways would her life change?

Her legs wobbled beneath her. She sank to the grass at the edge of the road, thankful that none of her neighbors were out and about. She hoped that the news didn't reach home before she did.

After a minute, she picked herself up and kept going. That was what life was about, after all. Making the wisest choices you could and moving forward.

How wise this choice would prove, only time would tell. All she knew was she could not refuse when the man responsible for the welfare of her country pleaded with her to do her part. Not just any man, but the wise and gentle man that she had talked with and listened to for hours. The man who in some small way, had reminded her of her own father.

The rest of her walk melted away before her

swirling thoughts. Her simple home came into view, her littlest siblings playing in the yard and, still, she could not explain why she had made that choice.

Jenna's mother took the news as well as Jenna had. She turned white and had to sit down. Jenna made her a cup of tea.

"How...?" said her mother, "Why?"

"I don't know," said Jenna.

"I always knew one of you would probably move away," her mother said, "But I thought it would be your brothers, years from now, with jobs or an education. And you have such a gift with people but... this Jenna? I just don't know."

"Me either," said Jenna, "I don't know what will happen. I may be home before you know it. I'll be fine, however it goes."

"Oh, Jenna," her mother shook her head, "how will we tell your siblings?"

"Maybe... just tell them I'm going to the castle because the king wants me to meet his son. We can tell Alana and Brandon more if they ask."

"They'll ask," said her mother.

~*~*~*~

Her mother helped her pack. There wasn't much she needed to take. She took her best dress and a few special things. Then her family walked her to the inn.

Jenna said goodbye with a smile on her face. The littlest of her siblings were excited, asking about bandits and knights and princesses. She promised to write them and tell all about her adventures. Her mother and Alana cried a little. Brandon was solemn.

Finally, when the soldiers had had about all they could take, Jenna climbed into the carriage that had been brought for her and they set off.

The palace was a long day's ride from her town. Jenna spent the day quietly in the carriage paying little attention to the scenery. She thought about her father. She thought about her mother and home.

SHALYNN MELLERUP

When the sun began to set, the whole company stopped at an inn to eat. Jenna slipped away for a walk and then waited in the carriage. She declined the king's offer to have food brought but thanked him for his concern. She reassured him that she wasn't dying, when he looked so worried. Within the hour they continued.

It was well after dark when they reached the palace. Torches lit the walls. The walls towered above them, dark and forbidding. Yet Jenna did not fear the building. It was only stone, no matter what it held. But she was afraid.

Chapter 4

As they entered the gate the soldiers fanned out to dismount. Boys and young men came forward to take the horses. The king dismissed all but half a dozen of his men. Soon the courtyard was nearly empty.

A tall, stern-faced woman came from the palace as the king himself helped Jenna from the carriage.

"Courage, daughter-of-a-king," he whispered.

She smiled uncertainty at him. Then she turned to face her future with her head held high. The woman curtsied low before the king.

"My Lord, you sent for me?" said the woman.

She spared only the shortest of suspicious looks for Jenna.

"Yes," said the king. "Prepare a room. I've found a bride for my son."

Jenna's clothes were clean but countrified and marked her as common. She was not nobility, nor royal. The woman glanced past her to the closed carriage.

"Yes, my Lord," she said.

She didn't spare Jenna another glance. She curtsied again and rushed off.

The king started towards the doors but paused as Jenna hung back. His brow furrowed in concern. Jenna took a deep breath and followed. The palace guards, who had changed places with the half dozen soldiers, followed well behind.

In a parlor of sorts, a table was set with tea and cakes and a cheery fire brightened the hearth. A set of windows overlooked darkness. Far below, only a few small lights could be seen. Jenna poured herself a cup of tea and sat down with a sigh. The maid looked shocked.

The king hid a smile as he dismissed the maid. The butler stood by the door. Jenna closed her eyes savoring the tea.

"Jenna," the king said quietly, "I'm sorry this has all been so hard. I..."

Jenna slowly opened her eyes, "I know."

She smiled slightly, "Tommy and Stacey are calling this 'my grand adventure'."

The King recognized the names of her youngest siblings. He smiled too.

Heavy footsteps sounded and a stranger burst into the room. His hair was dark and tousled. His eyes glinted angrily.

"So, you've found me a bride, Father," he asked loudly. "Is she ugly enough to punish me?"

The king nodded for the butler to leave. The butler shut the door behind him. Jenna sat still and unnoticed. She observed.

"Tristan," the king began.

Tristan interrupted, "Or did you pick someone rich, afraid I'd squander the *family fortune*?" His voice dripped with sarcasm and disgust.

He finally noticed Jenna.

"Who's this? Her maid? She must be ugly then, not rich. No rich woman would allow her servant to dress in peasants' rags."

Jenna rose slowly. Her expression made even

Tristan hesitate in his speech. Jenna didn't take her eyes off him.

"I'm sorry, Sir. I'm not sure I can go through with this."

Confusion flashed across Tristan's features.

"Tristan," said the king, "meet your bride. I hope."

The anger returned, warring with disbelief, "You want me to marry a peasant!?!"

"Sir, please...," said Jenna. She finally looked over at the king, "I'm not sure...this is a good idea."

The king sent her a gentle smile, "Jenna? Do you remember what I told you? Do you remember why I asked you?"

Jenna gave a small nod.

Tristan recovered and shook his head in disgust, "That's the best you could find; a shy peasant that doesn't even want to be royalty? Put her back where you got her."

The king's face was hard, but his eyes were sad, "You," he told his son, "do not know how lucky you are."

"Lucky?" Tristan asked, "You expect me to marry a common peasant? A girl with no fortune, no manners, no political connections... what exactly do you hope to gain, beyond making me a laughingstock?"

"A heart," the king said quietly, "Kindness, compassion... wisdom..."

Tristan sneered.

"Sir," said Jenna, "would you have someone show me to my room now, please?"

"It may not be ready yet, Jenna."

"I don't mind."

The king considered her.

"Very well," he said.

The king turned away from his son and started toward the door. Jenna started to follow.

"Afraid to fight?" Tristan scoffed, "Aren't you going to stay and share some of your precious wisdom?"

Jenna turned, "And who am I supposed to fight? Whatever doubts or faults... this is not my fight, today. Fight it yourself." she said, "I have my own doubt-battles to fight and I'd rather fight them without... being here."

Then she swept from the room. The king called a maid to take her to her new room. Jenna followed, glad to leave the turmoil and ready to rest. She would be willing to sleep on rocks, if it meant having her own room right then.

~*~*~*~

The next morning, Jenna awoke slowly. The servants had just finished readying her room when she had arrived. Jenna had thanked them and shooed them out, ignoring the questions about when her mistress would arrive. She told them only that things would be explained, come morning.

And now it was morning. Jenna hoped the king didn't expect her to explain. She wasn't entirely sure anyone would *believe* her.

~*~*~*~

Jenna kept her eyes closed and enjoyed the soft bed and the warm covers. Last night she had fallen asleep before she could enjoy it. She knew, just from the brief glimpse she had had the night before, that the room was huge. Finally, curiosity made her open her eyes.

She drew in a breath. The room was a palace, itself. The stone walls were covered by tapestries, velvet curtains hung across wide windows, a cheerful fire in the fireplace softened the morning chill. Rugs covered every inch of the floor and were so thick that Jenna *knew* her feet would sink in, just by looking. What she didn't see was her bag.

Jenna bit her lip. Had they put it in the wrong room? There wasn't much she needed but neither was it something she cared to lose.

She didn't think she would need the clothes she had packed for very long. They weren't suited for nobility or palace life, even for a servant. By the size of her room, Jenna guessed that the king would have someone see to a new wardrobe. But her bag also contained a sketch of her family that Brandon had given her last year.

Jenna slid out of the bed. Her shoes and stockings still lay beside the bedpost where she had left them. She circled the room looking for her bag. She opened the drawers of the huge dresser. They were empty. She looked under and around every nook and cranny in the room. Nothing.

Finally, she climbed up on the bed and looked

around for a place she had missed. Her gaze settled on the door in the far wall. Not the door from the hall... was it possible there was more to her room?

She slid off the bed and walked over. She cautiously lifted the door handle and pulled it open. It led to an empty room. Well, it was mostly empty. There were hooks on the walls and trunks on the floor. The trunks were empty.

This time when she saw a door, she didn't hesitate to open it. It was another bedroom. This one was small and had no windows. It was bigger than the room she shared with her sisters but not by so much. Clean sheets were on the bed, the floor was swept, and there was a trunk. This time she found her bag.

Jenna was relieved. She also experienced a fresh wave of doubt. This wasn't going to be easy. This palace in her own country might as well be in a foreign land. She sighed.

Then she carried her bag back to the big room. She put it in the dresser. If she didn't put it there now, she wouldn't dare later.

She looked over at the sun streaming in the

window. She had slept late. She put her shoes on and went looking for breakfast.

The hall door opened easily. Jenna looked both ways, but no one was around. She hummed to herself... left or right? If she left her room, there was a good chance she would get lost. Her nerves peaked but her stomach grumbled. Left.

~*~*~*~

A few hallways later, Jenna was no closer to getting breakfast. In fact, she hadn't even seen another person. She was lost.

If she weren't so hungry, being lost wouldn't have been so bad. It would be good to know her way around and this was one way to figure it out. She almost ran into the girl coming out of the next room.

"Oh!"

The girl almost dropped the tray she was holding.

"I'm so sorry," Jenna said. "Are you ok?"

"Whew! I'm fine. The tray is empty anyway," the girl said.

As the tray balanced, the girl finally got a good look at Jenna. Her eyebrows shot up.

"Are *you* ok?"

Jenna laughed quietly, mindful of the empty halls.

"I'm lost. Could you tell me how to get to the kitchen?"

The girl shook her head, "You *are* lost. Come on, I'll show you. That's where I'm headed."

By the time they reached the kitchen, Jenna not only knew that the girl's name was Amy, but that she had a brother in the army and a grandmother and younger sister at home. Amy liked to talk and Jenna was easy to talk to. When they reached the kitchen, Amy introduced her to every staff member in sight. Most of them didn't stop to talk.

The staff, Jenna soon realized, were wearing uniforms. The staff just assumed that she was a friend of Amy's. Amy soon had to deliver another breakfast tray but Jenna was at home in any kitchen, even this one.

As Amy's friend, Jenna was soon fed. Then she was put to work. Stir that pot. Scramble those eggs. Wipe off the trays. Jenna worked alongside the staff willingly.

She was so willing that somehow she ended up helping other staff in other rooms. They put her to work dusting. She was glad to have her hands busy.

She also kept her head down. The nobility was going to be unhappy enough that the prince was betrothed to someone lacking a title. She didn't want to stir up trouble but, silly as it seemed, who knew if she would ever be allowed to clean again?

Jenna didn't know whether to moan or laugh when the king came around the corner with two other men. The two girls cleaning with her were alarmed. One of them quickly began dusting between Jenna and the noble party, doing her best to keep Jenna out of sight. It suddenly occurred to Jenna that letting someone who wasn't staff work, might be *a bit* outside of the rules.

Jenna was more worried about the king's reaction to seeing his son's betrothed sweeping the floor. It wasn't exactly the normal activity of a future queen. Being the future queen was something else she didn't want to think about.

She saw the moment he recognized her. To

her relief, an expression of amusement followed his shock. He walked around the corner without speaking to her. A moment later he was back.

"Jenna! What are you doing down here?"

The two maids jumped, badly.

"I was hungry," Jenna admitted with a smile, "I didn't know where breakfast was."

The dark-haired maid looked ready to pass out at Jenna's daring. The blond one's jaw had dropped. Her dust rag hung limp.

The king frowned, "I'm sorry. I didn't realize you would be up this early."

Jenna laughed and her eyes lit up, "Early, Sir? I haven't slept that late since last summer."

The king looked bemused.

"I'll be sure to have breakfast sent up earlier, then," he said.

Jenna dropped a curtsy with a smile. "Thank you, Sir."

The king finally noticed the maids behind her. He frowned at them but not unkindly. They leaped back into action dusting and sweeping.

"You have a busy day ahead of you," he said to

Jenna, "The dressmaker will be at your room soon. There are others for you to meet as well."

Jenna smiled nervously and nodded, "Right."

She paused. "Um... I don't actually know where my room is."

And the king laughed.

~*~*~*~

A half hour later, Jenna was safely in her room with a light breakfast tray. The tray sat on the table but Jenna sat in the middle of the huge bed. Her legs were folded beneath her and her eyes were closed. She was rested and alone. She wouldn't get a better chance to think things through.

The thing that worried her the most was the most obvious: the prince. She had met him. Jenna worked her fingers through her braid. He was tall and handsome. He was so... angry and harsh. He would resent being forced to marry her. That was no way to live.

How could she back out? The king seemed so sure his son wasn't ready to rule, at least not without her. Only what power would a queen really have? Could she make things better or would she make them worse?

What would the people think? Would they resent her too? Most people respected the king. Would they accept her as his decision? Would they believe he made the right choice for Tristan's bride? *She* certainly wasn't sure.

Would the nobility shun her when the king wasn't looking? The servants she had talked to this morning, would they hate her or would they be proud to know her? Jenna gave up trying to think things through and buried her head under a pillow.

A knock on her door brought Jenna out from under the pillow. It also brought the dressmaker and her two heavily laden assistants into the room. The dressmaker clucked as she looked around the room, ignoring Jenna. It seemed to be in approval of the decor.

"Can I help you?" Jenna asked.

The dressmaker took in Jenna's mussed hair and countryfied dress. Her eyebrows rose to her hairline.

"Hmph." She said, "I was told Prince's betrothed would be waiting for me."

Jenna felt slightly ill hearing that title out loud. It took a moment to force herself to respond.

"Yes, Ma'am."

The dressmaker gestured widely, "Well? Where is she?"

"Here," said Jenna, "I'm Jenna Longfellow."

It didn't connect in the dressmaker's mind at first. She stared blankly. Then she looked around again.

Jenna sighed inwardly, then attempted to clarify.

"I'm sorry if it's an inconvenience. I just haven't got the right clothes for palace life."

Behind the dressmaker, the assistants gaped. Understanding slowly dawned in the dressmaker's eyes.

"Your highness! I apologize! Your clothes led

me to believe you were common. I should have seen through it immediately."

"It's quite alright," Jenna said. "You were correct, I'm nothing more than a commoner. Shall we begin?"

The dressmaker gasped and began to look faint. One of the girls hesitated behind her as though to catch her. The other assistant began laying out samples of cloth, all the while sending rather fearful glances at Jenna.

"Sit down, please! You don't look well. Please!"

Jenna was mildly alarmed. She had expected the shock but... she didn't want the lady to faint. There just wasn't any easy way to put it.

The dressmaker visibly pulled herself together. She was still pale but her face was almost stoic. She called one of her assistants over and whispered something softly. The girl murmured her assent and rushed out the door.

"Very well," said the dressmaker, "let us begin."

They began. Measurements were taken, dress designs selected, and colors and fabrics chosen. Jenna was left out of the process as much as possible. Only once, when she was looking over a shoulder at a dress design, had she objected.

"No. If you make that dress, you'll have to raise the neckline."

"Your highness," the dressmaker had replied, rather annoyed that her expertise was being questioned, "it's the latest of fashions. You simply must trust my judgment."

"I trust your judgment on fashion, not modesty."

"Please be reasonable!" said the dressmaker, "The prince's bride cannot be seen in any less than the latest fashions."

"Yes, she can," said Jenna, "I'll not be seen in something so low-cut."

"Modesty," was the reply, "is the greatest enemy of fashion. It simply isn't the first consideration."

"It is now," said Jenna.

Chapter 5

The next few days were full of lessons for Jenna. Lessons on manners, silverware, history, dance, and so many other things. They were also full of shocked looks, disbelief, and whispers. Her new dresses, court dresses, didn't help. The fact that the king had chosen a commoner to be the prince's bride was the topic of many heated discussions.

The nobility was torn between two views. Some were inclined to believe that the king had a good reason for such a prank. Among these, only about half believed that the wedding would ever take place. Others felt that an injustice had been done to the nobility. They felt that to bring a commoner into their midst was absurd. They felt that the king should have chosen a bride for his son from among their own daughters.

The nobility, of course, were not the first to hear the news. The servants knew first, and they told their families and friends before they ever told their masters. This group of people, the working class, the commoners, had their own divided opinions.

Some believed that the king had a good reason. Maybe, he was granting the people a voice. Maybe, he was showing his son that people are people, no matter their rank. Speculation of why a commoner, and why 'this girl', ran wild among this group. Only about half of them, maybe less, believed the wedding would really take place.

Others were less kind, more suspicious. They said the king would make an example of her: showing that no commoner would ever be fit to marry into the royal family. Others said she was probably just some village idiot with a pretty face and that the king was as blinded by beauty as any other arrogant man.

Jenna knew what people would be thinking but for the first few days, lessons and fittings kept her too busy to worry much. She only had dinner with the king once and she didn't see Tristan at all. The servants seemed to be avoiding her as diligently as her fiancé. Some of her gowns were finished, a hand-maid was brought in.

The maid's name was Henny. She kept to herself and when she spoke it was in a near-whisper. It took her a few tries to speak loud enough for Jenna to hear, when she had to give Jenna a direction.

Towards the end of the week, Jenna received an invitation to breakfast. It read:

Jenna dear, I know there has been little time for discussions, as of yet. I would like to invite you to breakfast with Tristan and me tomorrow at 7 am. We have much to accomplish in the coming weeks and I'm sure you have questions. Nor have I seen enough of your smiling face these past few days.

It was signed with flourish, which for some reason made Jenna smile. When Henny heard the contents of the note, she was all a flurry with panic. Jenna chose not to worry.

The next morning, Jenna was guided to the breakfast hall by a servant who *positively* insisted that to be a few minutes late was all the fashion among nobility. Jenna had considered that briefly. Then she had told them she was not interested in that particular fashion. She made it to breakfast on time.

The king rose as she came into the room.

"Good morning, Jenna," he said.

"Good morning, Sir," she responded with a smile and a curtsy.

"You look tired," he said as she was seated at the table. "Are you well?"

"I'm not tired, really. I'm just..." she paused, "not used to all of this yet. I've been so busy."

"How have the lessons been?"

Jenna made a teeny tiny face and thought out her words, "I enjoy the chance to learn so many things but... most of my teachers don't seem sure whether they are babysitting or teaching. They don't trust you enough to believe I should learn palace manners. I think I would be lost if I couldn't read."

Tristan stormed into the room and seated himself without acknowledging his father or Jenna. He stabbed a bite of food on his plate.

The king frowned heavily, "You're having difficulty with your teachers?"

"Sir, I'd be surprised if they enjoyed teaching a commoner. I'll be fine."

Tristan spoke abruptly, "She'll never be accepted. You can give up this insane scheme."

"Congratulations, son, you've driven me to insanity."

~*~*~*~

Breakfast was understandably stilted. As they finished the king asked Jenna if she had seen the library. Jenna admitted that she had not, and the king volunteered his son as her escort.

"I will not!"

Jenna flinched, ever so slightly.

The king studied his son impassively. "It's a perfect opportunity to get to know your bride-to-be."

Suddenly a shuttered look came over Tristan's face. He stood and threw his napkin down on the table. Then, to Jenna's shock, he offered his arm. Jenna stood slowly and took his arm.

"Have a good day, Sir."

"And you, Jenna."

She sent the king a last panicked smile over her shoulder, begging silently for reassurance, as she and Tristan left the room.

~*~*~*~

They arrived in the library without a word. Jenna had been afraid to start a conversation. Yet as they entered the library Jenna couldn't stifle a gasp. She stared at the high ceiling and gold-plated shelves that went on and on.

Jenna nearly got ahead of Tristan when he stopped in the doorway, so entranced was she with the sight of all the books. He looked down at her, his expression carefully neutral, and suddenly she realized... he was tall. And handsome.

When he looked away, she followed his gaze to the librarian's desk and the librarian behind it. Jenna flushed. The librarian was obviously curious and here she was thinking about how tall Tristan was. Tristan ushered her away from the librarian and deep into the shelves.

Suddenly, Jenna found herself spun around

and cornered against the shelves. Tristan, with one hand on her arm, was staring angrily into her eyes.

"Just who do you think you are?"

Jenna was as disconcerted by his close proximity as his sudden show of anger. "What?"

His firm grip on her arm tightened and he scowled, "Oh, don't play innocent. A country peasant who manages to make the king pick her instead of someone from his own class must have some tricks up her sleeve."

He leaned in and lowered his voice, "And I intend to learn every one."

Jenna tried to inch away but was held in place by that hand.

"I don't know what you're talking about," she responded breathlessly.

"I want to know... why he picked... you."

Jenna, suddenly irritated by his tactics and his presence, huffed. She reached up and focused on prying Tristan's hand off her arm.

"Well, you could have just asked," she muttered crossly.

Tristan released her arm but remained where he was, scowling angrily.

"He picked me because I care about people."

Tristan let out a snort.

Jenna sighed, "If you really want the answer to that question, you should ask your father."

"I'm not asking him, I'm asking you."

"I know, but why ask me?"

Tristan favored her with a dark look, "Indeed, why ask the ignorant country commoner."

With that unfavorable comment Tristan walked away, leaving Jenna lost in a maze of books.

~*~*~*~

Hours later, Jenna was still in the library. After wandering the shelves for a while, thinking as much as looking at books, she settled down with a likely title in her lap. She had the faint notion that she had lessons today, but she had never had so many books to herself before.

So it was that the servant who found her, found her sitting in a circle of her own skirts reading. It was Amy. When Jenna looked up and saw Amy, she smiled so warmly that Amy's resolve to treat her as she would most nobility or royalty melted more or less instantly.

"Hoo-y! Your highness, you've got a good bit of the castle in an uproar," Amy declared, reaching down to help Jenna to her feet.

Jenna's smile evaporated, "I do?"

Amy patted her on the back, "You do. Henny didn't know where you were, nor the housekeeper, and sure as anything, no one was going to go to the king and admit they'd gone and lost the prince's betrothed after breakfast. Now if only we'd thought to ask the librarian, there'd a been an idea, but we didn't. So now you're late for one lesson and you've missed another one all together..."

Amy noted Jenna's increasingly distraught expression, "Don't you worry none. What could they possibly do to a member of royalty like yourself?"

Jenna sighed, "Throw me off a turret?"

Amy stopped and stared at her in shock. Then smirked.

"Well, they might try at that," Amy admitted, "But don't worry. You have more people behind you than you know."

~*~*~*~

The next day, Jenna discovered that a walk in the gardens had been added to her itinerary. Along with the discovery came a brief note from the king.

I have made arrangements for Tristan to meet you for a daily walk in the gardens so that you and Tristan may become better acquainted.

Jenna's stomach fluttered nervously. The last meeting hadn't gone so well.

~*~*~*~

The king summoned Tristan to his study to tell him of the garden walks with his bride-to-be. It did not go well.

"You did what?" Tristan howled, "Isn't it enough that you've ruined my future with an arranged marriage to a commoner? I'll be a laughing-stock. And now you expect me to spend my last days of freedom in her company?"

The king winced. He had hoped, despite Jenna's

caution and warning, that his son would not fight the idea so strongly.

"She is a lovely young woman. Her company should not be so insufferable."

"She is a commoner; ignorant, filthy, and low-born," Tristan hissed.

The king rose from his chair in anger, "She will soon be your wife! You will treat her with respect or I will choose a new heir!"

Tristan skin lost all color, "You would force me to marry her or forfeit the throne? You wouldn't dare."

"Wouldn't I?" growled the king.

Tristan fled. He left the room without speaking another word. The king collapsed into his chair. The magnitude of the threat he had just issued struck him, full force.

"My son," he murmured, "my son..."

~*~*~*~

Jenna chose not to be surprised that Tristan did not meet her. The king had informed her there was a chance he would not. Jenna had chosen to come anyway. The fresh air did her good. The sunshine was so much brighter than it ever was indoors. So, despite Tristan's absence, Jenna continued her daily walks in the garden with only the servants for company.

All too quickly, a date was set for the traditional engagement ball. For Jenna, it would also be her introduction to court. There was very little Jenna feared more than the introduction to these people who were sure to resent, if not outright hate, her. People who, if the marriage took place, would become her responsibility every bit as much as the country folk she had grown up with.

Almost a full week passed before Jenna saw Tristan again. Jenna was with her dance instructor and was having difficulty with a certain dance step. Tristan, oblivious to her schedule, took a shortcut through the room where they were working.

"Your Highness!" purred the instructor, "Wonderful, wonderful. You are an excellent dancer! Perhaps if you were to lead her through this step, I would be better able to instruct her, then."

To Jenna's surprise, Tristan actually stepped forward, put his hand on her waist, and led her through the move. A move that was flawless and in perfect harmony. He stared down at her with the oddest look on his face.

"Beautiful!" cried the dance instructor. "You have it, Lady Jenna."

Tristan released her and left with only a murmured farewell to the instructor. Jenna continued her lesson and danced the step that had given her such difficulty to perfection. And, brief though it was, Jenna took courage in that one moment when she and Tristan had been in harmony. She had to.

The day of the engagement ball arrived. Jenna had not seen Tristan since the dancing lesson. She wondered, not for the first time, if this engagement was a wise choice. If not for the certain indescribable sense of peace she felt when she considered marrying the prince, she would have backed out of her agreement with the king and gone home. Of course, if she hadn't felt that certain indefinable peace, she never would have agreed in the first place. She hoped.

She stood for a final fitting of her ball gown and marveled at the craftsmanship. The dressmaker left the room in a much better mood than she had arrived. Then the rest of her day was spent learning the titles and names and important information about the guests who were expected, memorizing the schedule, and rehearsing her entrance to the ball.

Then the preparations began. The layers and layers of skirts and things were put on. Then her gown was arranged over them. She began to feel like the main dish of a feast, the way Henny and the others fussed over her. Every fold of fabric had to lay *just so*.

Her hair was arranged about her face. Elaborate loops made the style seem as though it were in motion. However, Jenna refused to let them pinken her cheeks or smother her in perfumes. It just wasn't her. And as tempting as it was to try to appear as one of them, hiding her true self seemed like a bad way to start a relationship.

Finally, it was time. The ball had already begun, as the king had explained, to give folks who arrive fashionably late time to arrive. Music drifted up to her. She stood in a doorway off to the side of a sweeping staircase.

One last moment. She had one last moment to change her mind and flee to the country. One last moment to go home, back to the life she had always lived, working hard to put food on the table. One last chance to flee, thus humiliating the prince. She allowed a dry, little smile to sneak past her anxiety.

And then there was silence.

"Our Prince and his bride!" The announcer cried, and trumpets began to play.

And with that, Jenna stepped from the shadows and descended. The staircase was Y shaped, two arms sweeping down to join into one at the landing. She could see Tristan coming down the other arm of the stairs, but it seemed as blurry as a dream to her. They reached the landing and she took his arm. Jenna had the feeling her smile looked a bit sickly.

"Not used to so many faces, Princess?" Tristan asked dourly.

The comment had an odd effect on Jenna. It

reminded her of when her brothers would tease her. And suddenly the crowd looked more human.

Tristan felt her hand relax on his arm. He glanced down to see her staring out at the crowd with a little smile. A real smile.

She really had looked like a princess, strangely enough, coming down those stairs. Though he had made the comment to rile her. Her hair was pulled up in a courtly style, but she looked nothing like the rest and he couldn't tell himself why. *Only a peasant girl,* he told himself. But something about her wasn't letting those thoughts take root.

They reached the ball-room floor, and the first dance began. Their dance. Tristan remembered the dance lesson he had interrupted all too well. It had made him wonder why he was in such a hurry to be rid of her. If she weren't a commoner, he might have considered himself lucky with his father's choice.

As the dance began, Jenna found she didn't know where to look. Over his shoulder seemed unbearably rude and it didn't really help since she could still see his expression. Looking straight ahead left her staring at the button on his jacket.

Figuring out where to look was rather flustering. She finally just swallowed her nerves the best she could and looked up into his face.

He stared down into hers. Their eyes locked, his challenging, hers wide but her gaze steady. They swirled around the room, once again finding themselves in perfect harmony.

When the dance ended, Jenna was immediately busy fending off prying questions and gilded insults. She was glared at, laughed at, scolded, and pointedly ignored. All in the most polite of ways, of course.

Just when she thought she couldn't take any more, Tristan swept her off to the dance floor without so much as a word. When her nerves began to recover, she quietly thanked him. He nodded absently.

The pattern continued throughout the ball. He never looked her way and yet every time she thought she was done for, he was there escorting her out to the dance floor. Jenna was kept so busy, she never even noticed that the king was never there.

When Jenna finally fell asleep, her last thought

was of her brothers. They would be waking up for the day's work, anytime now. Anytime...

Chapter 6

Jenna woke later than she ever had in her life. Instead of calling for breakfast, she left a note for Henny and slipped out the door. The hallways were more empty than she had ever seen them.

She meant to go to the kitchen. She didn't mean to stay there, now that her identity was known, but she could find something easy to carry and eat... somewhere. Anywhere quiet and free of people.

A shaft of sunlight distracted her from her destination. She followed it out onto a long, open balcony overlooking the city. She took a deep breath, soaking in the sunshine and open spaces. The heights made her feel as if she could fly...

"You again."

Jenna started at the sound of Tristan's voice. She had a fleeting thought that he might just pick her up and heave her over the balcony and be done with it. Surely, not.

"Good morning..." she trailed off, not knowing how to address him. By what name do you call your betrothed who doesn't want to be your betrothed and who might throw you off a balcony at any second? She smothered that thought and scolded her overactive imagination.

"Good morning, your Highness."

He regarded her with a scoffing glare, "So, not going to call your betrothed by his name? Are you going to call me "Your Highness" for the rest of your life?"

She couldn't help it. She rolled her eyes to the sky as she turned away from him and back towards the view.

"No, your Highness. I promise I'll never call you that again, if we make it through the wedding."

He was taken aback. IF? Didn't this country girl consider him firmly in her snare? What in the world did she think was going to stop the wedding? "What do you mean *if*?"

She shot a guilty glance over her shoulder, "Um, *when* we make it through...?"

She trailed off and looked away. He leaned on the wall beside her so he could see her face. Frustrated. He was so frustrated. His whole life was nothing but games.

"Is this engagement just a trick? Will he pull some other bride out of his hat when he thinks I've learned my lesson?"

"No," she murmured, "He fully intends for us to marry."

"Then why "if"?" he demanded.

She sighed. He waited, his scowl getting harder.

"Why not? Because I want to do the right thing. Or maybe I'm afraid. Because I need to take this a day at a time..."

She trailed off then suddenly snapped, "I could die tomorrow and the wedding would never happen or I might live a full life married to someone who hates me. What would you choose?"

She gasped in horror, "I'm sorry. I shouldn't have said that."

Tristan stared at her incredulously. It sounded to him like she didn't want to marry him at all.

She rubbed her elbows as though to ward off

a chill and started backing towards the door, "I'm sorry...if I've said... I'll leave you alone now."

He wasn't going to let her go that easily. Oh, no. He blocked her path.

"What in the world are you talking about?"

Jenna mentally scolded herself for saying too much. The possibility of him throwing her over the railing was seeming more and more likely. But then, she never had been one to back down. She lifted her chin.

"I was going to find breakfast. Would you like to join me?"

Tristan stared at her incredulously, "You're not moving from this balcony until I know what's going on."

Jenna closed her eyes. How did she end up in this mess, again? *Surely*, she hadn't chosen all this on *purpose*.

She opened her eyes, "Will the short version do?"

"Try it."

"I was minding my own business when your father wandered off his bride hunt. We got talking, then next thing I knew, I had agreed to marry his son. And if all of this is a trick, I will happily walk home, today."

Anticipating his next thought, she held up her hand and continued, "And despite the fact I am no happier with this marriage arrangement than you are, I will not be the reason it ends. And please. Don't ask me why. Even I'm not sure why I agreed to all this."

She shook her head and tried to wedge past him, "If you'll excuse me, I haven't had breakfast yet."

He took a half step back. She stumbled and nearly tumbled into his arms, but he caught her and she caught her balance. She apologized and rushed away blushing. And even though he didn't want to be stuck with the girl, he felt the amusement of the moment trick a laugh out of him. She certainly was cute when she blushed.

Hours later, Tristan idly stared out over the city. Of all his father's crazy notions, this one took the cake. A prince married to a servant girl. Of all things. Already, the courtiers were laughing behind his back. Angry mutters and sly smirks, even to his face. And to get out of this mockery of a betrothal he would have to give up the only thing that had ever truly been his.

Maybe that had been his father's intention all along. Not to bend Tristan to his will and treat him as a puppet but to set before him a task so distasteful that no prince would do it. A plan to force him to give up his birthright.

Tristan's jaw stiffened in anger. Tricks. It was all tricks, no matter what the girl had to say, no matter what she even knew. Just tricks. He would show them. He would marry that girl. Someday he would be king and no trick of vanity would steal that away.

~*~*~*~

Why, oh, why had she been so silly? Rushing led to mistakes and mistakes led to... well, she supposed mistakes didn't normally lead to falling into the arms of handsome princes but why take the chance? Jenna mournfully wondered where all the good sense that the king had praised her for had gone to this morning.

Jenna finally found the kitchen and Amy kindly showed her the way back to her rooms. When Jenna told her about getting lost yet again, she also did her best to explain the lay-out of the castle as they went. Jenna kept the encounter with Tristan to herself.

To Jenna's surprise, Tristan did meet her for her daily walk in the gardens. He smiled but it didn't reach his eyes. His eyes glowed like the black-smith's forge.

"Would it be rude to ask why you decided to keep me company this morning?" Jenna asked.

Alarmingly, Tristan didn't answer. He plucked a rose from a nearby plant and handed it to her with a flourish. Jenna took the rose even as she leaned away from him ever so slightly.

Then he offered his arm. She gingerly reached out and took it and they proceeded around the garden. When they had walked for several minutes, she could take the silence no longer.

"What has gotten into you?" she finally cried.

"Beautiful day, isn't it?" he responded.

She didn't say another word. When they reached the castle again, he favored her with a bow and walked away. When the required chaperons, who were a good distance behind, finally caught up, one of them laid a comforting hand on Jenna's shoulder.

"Don't worry, my Lady, dear. We'll watch out for you."

But Jenna was too bewildered to respond.

~*~*~*~

The next day, it was Jenna who didn't show up for the walk in the gardens. Then came the knock on her door.

"Prince Tristan here to see you, Milady."

Jenna hurried over to take Henny's place at the door before Henny could let him into the rooms. Jenna peered around the edge. Tristan met her gaze with a dangerous smile and a flinty spark in his gaze.

"Coming, Princess?"

Still wary, Jenna didn't take her eyes off him as she called back over her shoulder, "Henny? I believe I'll be taking that walk after all."

Then she straightened her spine and stepped out to take his arm. They made it as far as the gardens before either one spoke.

"So, tell me about yourself," Tristan said, "Tell me about the woman I'm going to marry."

Jenna felt the heat rise to her face. She looked away.

"What would you like to know?"

"Hmm... you were a servant when you met my father?"

"Yes, though not like you are used to here. I

worked in an inn, serving food to the guests and other such things."

"How is that not like a servant here?"

"Perhaps it was the people who were different, more than the job," she allowed.

"Hmm."

"People from far off places would stop to spend the night, all of them tired. I'd serve them a warm meal, fill their mugs, listen when they talked... And most of them were happier people when they were done. Locals would stop in sometimes for a meal and they knew my name, and my family, and would ask after my mother or if my brothers were still in school..." she drifted off, at a loss for how to describe something she knew so well.

"So. You have a family."

"Yes, I have a family."

"Tell me about them."

"Forgive me, Tristan, but I don't trust you enough to tell you that."

A strange expression crossed Tristan's face.

"Wait," she amended. "Wait. I can tell you some."

She paused, looking down at the grass to collect her thoughts.

"My mother is the best cook I know. She taught my sisters and I everything she knows. I have a little brother with a fondness for toads. I have a sister whose stitch work is as beautiful as your castle tapestries."

"And what did they think of you coming to marry me?"

She sent him a sideways glance. "Are you sure you want to know?"

He frowned, "Of course."

She huffed a nervous laugh, "Well. My youngest siblings thought it was very exciting. They expect me to bring home stories of brave knights and beautiful ladies. We haven't told them I'm getting married. Not yet."

Sadness washed across her face before she continued.

"The others...I suppose, the best way to say it is that they fear you. They're afraid... that my decision... will bring me a lifetime of heartaches."

She faded off by the last word, so quiet he barely heard her. Then she straightened and put a bright, if somewhat fragile, smile on her face. "It's a beautiful day, isn't it?"

"Hmm."

~*~*~*~

Tristan found himself reluctant to leave her side, for once. The more he learned about her, the more confused he became as to what she was gaining. The things that seemed like such obvious benefits to him, didn't seem to matter to her. If she could be believed, she didn't even want to go through with the arrangement.

Of course, he had no reason to believe her.

"So, tell me, what do you gain from going through with this?"

She turned and looked him in the eye as though gauging his meaning. "You mean like money?"

He nodded, "Yes. Money or land... or are you after the position, alone?"

A tiny smile crossed her face, "Not the position. I've never envied people like you. Having to deal with diplomats and foreign powers?"

She shook her head, "Do you realize, every time

a war starts or people die of starvation, everyone blames the king? I never looked for that responsibility. It never even crossed my mind that I might gain it by accident!"

She sighed and bit her lip thinking, "As for what I gain... I suppose... my brothers have the money for schooling now, but that money was a gift before..." she swallowed, "your father approached me about marrying you."

She spread her skirts, "I have these lovely dresses. And I've made new friends since coming here. And the library, I've never seen so many books! But now I'm just counting my blessings."

She smiled sadly, "I'll tell you what I'll lose, though, if you'd like."

Confusion flitted across his face, "By all means. Do. What is it that you lose?"

"Privacy, for one. Between servants, chaperones, and instructors I haven't been truly alone since I've been here. And my family. I have no idea when I'll see them again."

"You could bring your family here."

"They will be happier where they are. I want that even more than I miss them."

She took a breath, "And I miss my freedom. At home I could go anywhere and do anything I chose. My siblings and I would go out for hours without telling anyone at all. We'd go for walks and visit friends and swim..."

The thought of Jenna soaking wet caught Tristan off guard. Jenna didn't even notice.

"And do you know what else I miss? I miss baking with my sisters and helping mama with dinner and sweeping the floor." Her voice choked up, "Of all the things to miss! If I picked up a broom here, or came to dinner with flour on my face, I'd probably cause a diplomatic incident."

A tear slid down her face and she swiped it away, "I'm sorry. Would you excuse me?"

Then she turned and very nearly ran for the palace.

~*~*~*~

The next day, when Jenna went to the garden, Tristan was waiting there with saddled horses.

Tristan looked down from his majestic mount. "Today, we will ride out into the countryside instead of walking the gardens. I had a lunch packed for later."

The corner of Jenna's mouth inched up in a smile, "At home we would call that a picnic."

Tristan shrugged carelessly. "Very well. A picnic then."

When Jenna made no move to mount the other horse, he frowned haughtily and sarcastically added, "What? Not coming?"

Jenna looked up at him with a funny little smile.

"Tristan, I never learned to ride."

A look of confusion flitted across his face for a moment. Then he flashed a dashing smile, expertly maneuvered his horse to her side, and offered a hand.

"Then you shall have to ride with me."

With a rather skeptical quirk to her smile, Jenna took his hand and gasped as he lifted her off the ground and into the saddle behind him.

"Wrap your arms around me."

Jenna quickly did as he instructed. If she held on a little too tight? It was only because she was afraid she would fall. But Tristan found he didn't mind in the slightest.

"Off we go!"

~*~*~*~

As she caught sight of the picnic site, Jenna gasped in delight. A beautiful meadow spread out before them. A small, tree-bordered creek ran along the edge adding the natural music of running water. The moment Tristan swung her down from the horse, she was running, dancing, through the grass.

As Tristan handed off his horse to the groom, he couldn't help but be entranced by the spectacle. Sunlight made every shining highlight in her hair glow and her face was lit up as bright as the day as she exclaimed with delight over the meadow and the trees and the brook. It had never crossed Tristan's mind that a person could be *delighted* over those things.

A trickle of unease shot through him. No girl of nobility would dance in a meadow.

"Where shall I set up the picnic, your Highness?"

Tristan swung his distracted gaze towards the groom, "Hmm? Oh. Just over there."

Tristan followed her as she skipped her way toward the creek. Suddenly remembering her audience, Jenna stopped dancing and smiled shyly.

"Thank you for this," Jenna said. "I've missed being out of doors."

Neither the smug charm of the last few days nor the resentful anger of when she first met him, could be seen on his face. No, he just looked confused. Bewildered. The perplexed expression didn't leave his face as he answered, either.

"You're welcome."

For a brief moment, they simply stared at one another. Then he offered her his arm and they strolled across the meadow just as though it were another palace garden.

Chapter 7

The knock on the door of the king's rooms that night caused him to pause. As late as it was no man should have cause to disturb him. Having dismissed his manservant earlier in the evening, the king called out.

"You may enter."

His eyebrows rose when his son entered. It was the first time in years that his son had sought him out in his rooms.

"Tristan!"

His son regarded him with a lowered brow and an odd expression.

"Father."

"Come! Sit!"

Tristan reluctantly settled into a chair by the

fire. The king held his silence, waiting for him to speak. Finally, in a low voice, he did.

"I think I begin to see why you chose her for me. She's not like the other girls, is she?"

Frowning he continued, "You shouldn't have done it, though. She shouldn't have to marry me."

The king sighed, "I gave her a choice, you know. She chose to come."

Tristan eyed him skeptically. "What did she say, when you asked her?"

The king chuckled, "She didn't say anything, at first. She swooned."

Tristan smiled, "No..."

His father chuckled again, "Oh, yes. But don't tell her I said so."

Tristan frowned again. "You shouldn't have asked her."

His father sighed wearily, "You may be right but she was everything I wanted you to find in a wife. Warm. Bright. Honest..."

For a long moment both father and son were silent, staring at the flames in the fireplace. The fire was as cozy in its gilded frame as the fire of any humble home.

The king shook his head, "I searched among every noble household in our entire kingdom and I found no one worthy. But Jenna..."

The king fell into silence again, unable to find the words to tell his son what he wished to. That not only was this simple girl worthy of being a queen but also that this girl was a girl to love and treasure. A girl that he loved as a daughter from the moment she spoke. A girl that he had felt could love Tristan and that, somehow, Tristan might love her too.

Since he could find the words for none of these things, he was silent. Yet somehow, even heavy with unspoken words, the silence was a comfortable one. So, after some time, Tristan spoke again. And as they had never done before, they talked late into the night.

~*~*~*~

The next day as Jenna and Tristan walked in the garden, Tristan was unusually reflective. He was quieter... thoughtful. And as she left for her own rooms, Tristan laid a hand on her arm.

"Jenna..."

She paused and looked back.

"...Thank you."

A question creased her lovely brow.

"My father and I are speaking again and I know that it's because of you."

Her expression hinted that she might argue that point, but he shook his head.

"No, don't argue. Though I don't know how, it is because of you."

Before she could think what to say, he smiled and was gone.

~*~*~*~

That afternoon, Jenna had the first fitting for her wedding dress. It was actually a beautiful gown. Still Jenna was relieved when the fitting was over. The dressmaker was no more Jenna's favorite person than Jenna was the dressmaker's.

And the gown... the feel of the silk draped over her shoulders... the thought of the time it would be worn...

Jenna had never been a girl prone to panic, but

she felt her lungs getting tight. One moment she would remember the Tristan of the picnic in the meadow and would begin to relax. The next, she would remember the arrogant Tristan of their first meeting and her shoulders would tense up and the dressmaker would stick Jenna with a pin.

After such a miserable hour, Jenna was ready for honey in her tea and a snack. Instead of ringing for the servants now at her beck and call, she slipped away from Henny and went on her own two feet. Still, it was with some hesitation that she poked her head in the kitchen.

As she had feared would happen, the kitchen dissolved into chaos the moment she was spotted.

"Princess Jenna!" cried the head chef.

A flustered underling dropped a pan with a bang. Serving maids and cooks scrambled to line themselves into some kind of order or disappeared entirely.

"How can we help you?"

"Just a cup of tea," Jenna answered quietly.

"Of course! Right away. And where would you like to take your tea?"

Jenna finally spotted Amy in the back of the

room. Their eyes met, Amy's cautious and concerned, Jenna's tentative. Still holding Amy's gaze, Jenna answered the chef.

"The library, if you please. In the nook by the windows."

"Very well. And shall I... shall I have someone escort you there?"

Again, Jenna looked to Amy, then away.

"No thank you," she said.

~*~*~*~

A few minutes later, a footman delivered the tray to the library. Jenna thanked him but made no move to eat. Her appetite was gone.

As the footman's steps echoed across the vast room and faded away. Jenna stared out the window. A movement behind one of the shelves caught her eye. Amy moved out from behind the books.

A glad smile, a relieved smile, swept over Jenna's face. Amy tentatively smiled too.

"Amy! Do you have a few minutes?"

"Yes... Princess."

Jenna looked alarmed. The look faded to

resignation and then settled to something else. Something serious and open and beseeching, all at once.

"I'm not the Princess yet, Amy. And even if I were...I mean...when I am... I hope I can still count you as a friend?"

With that, Amy smiled.

"Of course, you can. I just didn't think the future queen would really care to associate with servants."

"But you still came?"

"Well," Amy said, "that's what my head said but something else was telling me to come."

"Thank you."

It was late afternoon before Amy returned to her duties. But, as she assured Jenna, she was well caught up with her work and wouldn't be missed. The conversation, though, lingered in Jenna's mind.

"Which Tristan do you think is the real Tristan?" Jenna had asked.

"Oh, I suspect they're both real. It's just different sides of the same coin."

"Yes, but which way will the coin fall?"

Amy didn't really have an answer for that but she did have a comment.

"Maybe it doesn't really matter, if you're marrying him either way."

She had paused, then. Taken a sip of tea.

Then she added, "I'm glad you love him. He probably needs a bit of love, more than most."

Then Jenna had let the subject drop.

~*~*~*~

Jenna wanted her mother. She missed the wise advice and comforting hugs. But, for the fact of neither her mother nor her sisters being there, Jenna was thankful for her friendship with Amy. It had been a comfort and Jenna had woken feeling hopeful.

The hopeful feeling had continued when she had received an invitation to breakfast, not from the king but from Tristan. To her delight, the breakfast was to be served not in the dining room but by the gardens.

~*~*~*~

Tristan stalked to the window and looked out, then paced back across the room to stare at his reflection in the mirror. This breakfast had been his idea but, suddenly, he wasn't sure. He should send her home. Convince his father that she would be better off in her own provincial village and that he, Tristan, would be fine without her. Frustrated, he ran a hand through his hair.

~*~*~*~

Tristan was late. Jenna toyed with the cup of tea that she had finally allowed a servant to pour for her as minutes passed and he didn't arrive. Perhaps this breakfast was merely a means to prove he didn't care. That he had more important things to do.

The thought hurt her more than she wanted to admit. She wanted to believe that she was strong enough, wise enough, not to be hurt by someone else's perception. But, against her better judgment, she did care and it did hurt.

As she resigned herself to the fact that he had probably done exactly that, he came around the corner. He bowed over her hand, a smile on his lips, a shadow in his eyes.

"Sorry I'm late."

"Is everything alright?"

"Yes, of course..."

Jenna knew better. But sometimes, it was better not to push a matter. Something in her heart was telling her that this was one of those times.

~*~*~*~

Tristan walked in the garden. He had places to go and people to meet but they would have to wait. By all rights, breakfast should have been a stilted affair, after his rude late arrival and with the untruth that everything was alright, hanging over his head. But instead, Jenna had pulled back. Not shutting herself off but merely subsiding into a companionable silence.

His own silence had been less than companionable. The space she gave him had forced him to think and, as he sat across from her, he didn't like the conclusion that he was drawing. He didn't want her to go. It was selfish. It went against all he had once believed in his arrogance but he wanted her by his side.

Could he allow her to marry him knowing it was arranged? Could he deprive her of the simple life she so obviously treasured, merely for his own sake? Yet she had agreed, sight unseen, to marry him. He could have been hideous, for all she knew, yet she had agreed to marry him. Because his father asked it of her. For her country.

For her country, he mused. Certainly, his county would be better off with her as their queen. Perhaps, he couldn't ask her to marry him for himself but for her county? She would do it for love of her county and respect for her king.

Then what? Would she grow to hate him? Love him? His heart kicked in his chest. Could she grow to love him? Despite the circumstances?

Chapter 8

Jenna fingered the white lace and slid her hand over the flow of the skirt. It was finished. The seamstress had left the dress against her wishes, warning Jenna not to touch it and carefully wrapping it in a protective layer of cloth. That layer of cloth now lay draped across the bed as Jenna stared at her wedding gown.

Carefully, she unhooked it from where it hung and held it up against herself. She didn't look in the mirror. The final fitting, the image of herself in this dress... wasn't something she would ever forget. She had looked in the mirror and wondered. As people had looked at her father and seen a man with a kingly heart, would they be able to look at her and see the heart of a princess?

Because if she wore this dress, she would surely need one. She would have a people to serve and protect. She would have a husband to love who might not know how to love her in return. A father-in-law who would need encouragement. And her husband, someday he would be king and she would have to be there to support him in that. She would need more than the heart of a princess; she would need the heart of a queen.

Jenna sighed. Picking up the cloth cover, she wrapped the dress just as carefully as the dressmaker, herself, had. Then she went over to the window and stared out over the hills. Time was passing so quickly. Her wedding was only a month away.

"Mama, I miss you," she whispered. But the wind swept her words and her tears away.

~*~*~*~

"Jenna?" said the king, "Do you have a moment?"

For the king, Jenna would always have a moment to spare. Besides, anything that would interrupt the never-ending lesson on foreign policy was doubly welcome.

"Of course," Jenna said.

Her tutor took his cue and excused himself from the room. The king settled in the chair across from Jenna. No longer focused on her lesson book, Jenna was once again able to appreciate the room that had been set aside for her education. The furniture was cozy, the desk against the wall provided a perfect place to do her written work, and large windows flooded the room with light.

But because people are more important than rooms that can be redecorated at a moment's notice, Jenna gave the king her full attention. This was more than just a visit, she realized. He had come with some news to share.

"Jenna, I have had reports lately, and many of them, on people's reaction to this wedding."

He stood again, a serious frown on his face, "There has been more of a reaction than I anticipated."

Noticing her concern, he shared a little smile.

"It's not all bad. In fact, the people seem to have rallied around you as their champion. They like the idea of one of their own marrying into royalty. The fact that I was the one who chose you rather than Tristan has helped matters, sadly enough."

"But that isn't what worries you, is it?" Jenna asked.

"No, I shouldn't be worried. Tristan had agreed to the wedding. But... there are those among the people who don't believe that the marriage will happen. They think it is merely a political ploy to gain their favor and there are those who are using the opportunity to stir up trouble. I'm afraid if the wedding were to be called off or even delayed for any reason, there would be... civil unrest. A revolt even."

Jenna decided that she preferred foreign policy to current politics.

"What about among the nobility? Is the reaction so strong there, too?"

This time the king really did smile.

"To my surprise, no. You have won over a good many people, Jenna. There will always be murmurs but the majority of them seem to have accepted you."

Shaking his head at his own concern, the king said, "Don't let the worrying of an old man concern you. The people love you. Tristan seems to be fond of you."

"Even your tutors in this subject speak highly of you and your progress," he said, "and don't think I've forgotten what a chore it is to learn foreign policy. It was my least favorite subject."

"I'm sorry, Jenna my dear. I only meant to give you some idea how the people were taking all this, not to worry you."

He looked so sorry that Jenna smiled.

"Thank you, sir," she said, "I appreciate knowing these things."

And she truly meant it. Even if the talk of a revolution in her name was startling. She only hoped that that sort of talk would die out, and quickly.

~*~*~*~

Tristan wanted to woo the girl he was going to

marry. She was going to marry him and he wanted her to be glad of it. Only, how did he show her...

How did a man go about it? He had had more than his share of female attention but he was under no illusion that they cared for him. He could see through them; all they saw was a prince. Jenna, wouldn't see a prince at all. Just... him.

Flowers? But the gardens were full of flowers that she saw every day. Chocolate? Did she even like chocolate? He had never asked nor noticed.

Unable to think of an original idea, he sought out his father. He had faced this. Hadn't he? Unlike most royal marriages, his parents' marriage had not been arranged. At least, not officially.

He knocked on the door of his father's office. From inside, his father's voice called for him to enter.

"Tristan!"

His father was surprised to see him and rightly so. It was the first time he had come to his father's office like this... perhaps ever. Suddenly uncomfortable asking what he had come to ask, Tristan was none too quick to enter the room.

"Are you busy?"

"Yes," his father answered, "But I have a minute. I wanted to speak to you anyway. Did you want to ask me something?"

"It was nothing."

The king raised a questioning brow but didn't ask again. If his son had come, it was enough for now that he had meant to seek his father's company or council. He didn't want to push him away. Next time, perhaps, he would be comfortable saying what he meant to say.

"Very well. I was coming to tell you I'm leaving for a few days."

The announcement was no surprise to Tristan. While most things could be handled from the castle, the occasional business had always called his father away.

"How long will you be gone?"

"Less than a week, if all goes well. No more than that."

Tristan nodded and turned to leave. As he reached the doorway, an idea occurred to him. It was unusual and it wouldn't be easy to achieve. Almost certainly, it wouldn't be done before the wedding but it was a start.

"Are you sure there's nothing you wanted to ask me?" his father asked.

"No. It was nothing."

As if to prove it so, Tristan smiled.

"Travel safe," he said.

Chapter 9

Jenna had a funny feeling Tristan was fishing.

"Of all the things you like best, what are your three favorites?"

It was an odd question to begin with. What "of all things" did he mean? He was just trying to get to know her better, he claimed. So, Jenna was trying.

"I like..." She closed her eyes to better think.

"I like cold spring mornings when the land is covered in fog and the sunlight is just beginning to burn it away. And... I like the sound of the brook that runs through the forest. And..."

She thought hard. Favorite things. She had so many.

"And hearing the sound of gentle rain and just

knowing that when I go out the next morning the garden is going to be full of new growing things."

She smiled up at him. Tristan looked back at her bemused. Jenna doubted that was exactly what he'd had in mind when he asked the question.

"Is that all?" he asked.

"Well, you said three," said Jenna.

"I did, didn't I?" he shook his head. "It just couldn't be simple and normal like roses or chocolates, could it?"

Jenna glanced at him from under her lashes. Roses or chocolates? Is that what he was fishing for?

"I like both," she assured him.

Then cheerfully added, "as well as peppermint candy and fresh raspberries from the garden."

"Ah-ha!" he murmured, looking for all the world as if he'd solved a mystery.

Jenna mentally added another favorite to her list... that smile.

~*~*~*~

Jenna met Amy by the palace herb garden. The library had become their usual meeting place but today the sun was shining and neither of them wanted to be inside. So instead, they were here.

"You look happy," Amy commented.

"Do I?" said Jenna.

"You do," Amy confirmed, "What happened?"

"He wanted to know what I liked. He wanted to know if I liked roses and chocolates."

"He did?" Amy asked, "Really?"

"Really," Jenna answered.

Amy reached over and gave Jenna the biggest hug she could muster.

"I'm so glad for you."

Jenna smiled tentatively.

"It's a little early to get excited," she said, "but I'm... hopeful."

"I think our prince has good taste," Amy teased. "He's picking you..."

"And you should ask him about those little chocolates with cream inside," she added.

Jenna laughed.

~*~*~*~

Tristan was waiting the next morning at breakfast.

"How would you like to go riding?" he asked.

"A ride?" asked Jenna, "Where?"

"And how?" She added, "I still can't ride you know."

"I know," Tristan agreed affably. "We'll have to remedy that one of these days."

In Jenna's opinion, it didn't sound as if he were in a great deal of a hurry to actually do anything about it. However, if he wanted to make an effort to spend time with her, she wasn't about to argue.

"I thought we'd ride down through the city," Tristan said. "It occurred to me you haven't seen much of it."

"That's true," she agreed, "I'd be happy to go."

"Good," said Tristan, leaning back in his chair. "Good."

~*~*~*~

Around midday, Jenna met Tristan in the courtyard. He gave her an appreciative glance and Jenna blushed. Soon they were seated on the same big horse they had ridden on the day of the picnic. Jenna made sure the skirts of her new riding habit were situated.

"Ready?" asked Tristan.

Jenna wrapped her arms around his waist. "Ready."

~*~*~*~

The streets of the city were full of life. It was so much like the narrow streets of her home village with its bustle and noise, but so much more. The same sounds of people buying and selling, telling tales, and rushing, but it was louder and stronger and overwhelming.

Tristan maneuvered his tall horse through the crowds with practiced ease. Jenna found herself thankful for the height of the horse that put her above the crush of the crowd. As people recognized their prince, the path cleared more.

Some used that as a way to push towards Tristan, hawking their wares, but most of the crowd was content to observe. Jenna suspected sighting the prince was common enough here but her presence was adding to the novelty. She could hear the whispers moving in behind them as they passed.

Suddenly, there was a change in the crowd. A murmur, a sense that something was about to happen, and in that lull in the wave of voices a voice shouted out above the crowd.

"Long live our queen!"

The rising tide of voices took up the cry, "Long live our queen!"

"A princess of the people!" someone shouted.

"A princess of the people!"

Jenna could feel the color draining from her face. She was glad for the shelter of Tristan's back, even as he tensed. Never had the phrase "daughter of a king" had such meaning.

Drawing on the strength of that honorary title she unfisted her hand from where she had unconsciously gripped Tristan's tunic and lifted her hand in greeting to the crowd. They roared their approval, pressing closer. Tristan turned, looping his arm around her waist.

"Trust me," he murmured.

"I do," Jenna said.

Then Tristan pulled her from sitting behind him to sitting cross ways on the saddle in front of him. Cradling her back against one arm, he lifted the other in a celebratory fist.

"To my future bride!"

For a moment the crowd faltered, unable to believe that their prince had so publicly claimed his common bride. Then, one by one, they took up the cry until the whole crowd roared.

"Our prince's bride!"

Jenna, feeling much braver in Tristan's arms, waved and even managed a smile. Pushing and shoving, they sang and cheered. They reached out to touch Jenna's skirt and shouted their congratulations to Tristan. The joyful mob followed them all the way back to that palace gates.

As the gates closed behind them, Jenna leaned against Tristan's chest with a shuddering sigh. They rested there for a moment. Those who had come from the castle hearing the noise hung back at the slight shake of Tristan's head.

Tristan walked the horse around to the relative privacy of the stables. When Jenna still made no move to get down, he shifted his shoulder to better see her face.

"Are you all right?"

"I have never been more terrified in my life," Jenna stated emphatically.

But she took a deep breath and slid off the horse. Tristan dismounted behind her.

"They meant you no harm," he said.

"For a moment I wasn't sure they were so harmless towards you," Jenna answered, "And there were so many of them! But you turned that around beautifully with what you said."

She cast a tentative glance towards him, followed by a small smile. She stepped away.

"I think I'll head to my rooms and rest."

Tristan nodded his acknowledgment. As he watched her walk away and handed his horse off to the groom, he removed his gloves. And he wondered that his own hands were not shaking.

Chapter 10

It had been a week since the king had left. He had been expected back sooner than that, but Jenna supposed that it wasn't usual for a king's business to take longer than expected. Tristan didn't seem worried. But then, he hadn't brought up their ride to the village either and that had been an unnerving experience even if there *hadn't* been any real danger.

It had been a few days since their ride into the village but Jenna couldn't get it out of her mind. Had the people, the people that she had been one of since birth, really chosen her as their champion? Tristan, she could now see, had the makings of a great king. Why could they not rally behind him instead?

Feeling the need to see Tristan for herself, she

asked one of the servants about his whereabouts and made her way to the study near the library where she was told she could find him. She raised her hand to knock on the heavy oak door but it swung open at her touch.

"Tristan?" she called.

"Jenna?" he answered incredulously, "Is that you? Is everything alright?"

He rose from his desk, leaving the papers he had been reading behind. Jenna glanced down shyly.

"Everything is fine. I... just wanted to... see you."

Surprised but pleased, Tristan smiled. If she was seeking him out for no reason, then maybe his plans to woo her stood a chance.

"I'm working but if you'd like to stay, I can leave the door open."

"Oh!" said Jenna, "The door was already unlatched, it just swung open when I knocked! I didn't mean to intrude."

Tristan reached out and took her hand, leading to an overstuffed chair to sit down.

"I know," he said, "I'm glad you came."

~*~*~*~

An hour later, Jenna was still in the chair. She had left long enough to find a book in the library and then returned to keep Tristan company. The occasional scratch of Tristan's pen registered in her mind along with the soothing smell of ink and paper.

The story in her hand slowly drew her in until even the curious servant peering through the open doorway failed to garner her notice. Tristan smiled to himself as he noted the strand of hair that had come loose and fallen over her forehead and the way she had tucked her feet up under her without even noticing she had. She was still lost in the story when the messenger found them.

"Sire," he said, falling to one knee, "Your Majesty. We have received word that your father's party was attacked. He has disappeared."

Jenna's book tumbled to the floor unnoticed. The messenger noticed her for the first time. He hesitated. However, Tristan remained focused on him.

"His men?"

"All accounted for, sire. Healing at a nearby inn."

"And where was my father last seen?"

"One of the men saw his horse spooked during the attack. They followed but a rainstorm caused them to lose the tracks. When they found the king's horse it was climbing out of a swollen river."

The messenger swallowed hard as he prepared himself to deliver the final blow, "Sire, when last seen the king was badly wounded. He is missing, presumed dead."

Tristan's complexion visibly paled. Jenna let out half a sob, then rose to stare out the window. She clutched her arms around her waist, holding herself together.

"Are you certain?" Tristan asked sharply.

"Nearly certain, sire. His men searched for days and found no trace of him."

The chief advisor of the king's council appeared in the doorway. With the wave of a hand, he dismissed the messenger. The messenger glanced to the prince for approval but the prince was staring into space. With a short bow, the messenger obeyed the unspoken order and gratefully left the room.

"Your Majesty, I heard the news. Your father will be greatly missed."

Tristan gave a sharp nod, his jaw tight with suppressed emotion. The chief advisor motioned to Jenna and then the door with the silent suggestion that he dismiss her, but Tristan shook his head. The advisor sighed heavily.

"I wish it wasn't so but there are decisions that need to be made," he said.

Tristan nodded.

"We will need to set a date for your coronation. Plans will need to be made for a memorial service. You also will be able to call off the wedding, or postpone it indefinitely, if you prefer."

"No!"

Tristan felt his heart leap with joy at Jenna's exclamation. But she did not turn from the window. Her shoulders bunched tightly, her arms crossed about her waist. As she remained there, his heart sank again. He waited.

Jenna's eyes were wide with horror. Had she really just said that? The word had torn from her throat involuntarily when the advisor had mentioned calling off the wedding. It would be grief on top of grief if she lost Tristan too.

But... there was a logical reason not to put off the wedding, too. As she pondered it, she was sure. Carefully schooling her face, she turned to face the men.

"If you postpone the wedding, or call it off, people will die. They'll riot, maybe even revolt. Tristan," she appealed, "you remember how they were. The day you took me into town."

Tristan's face was expressionless, but he nodded, "The wedding will continue as planned. In my father's honor."

Though his chief advisor looked less than pleased at the concept, he could see the wisdom in the decision. Honoring his father's last wishes would place the prince in high esteem as he began his reign. Nor would it be unwise to gain the people's favor.

"As you wish, your Highness," he conceded, "As you wish."

~*~*~*~

Tristan was gone. As soon as he had been able to escape, he had taken his horse from the stables. No one had heard from him in the hours since. Jenna didn't expect he would be back before dark.

She had retreated to her room at first. Then realizing how thin a door separated her from her maid, Henny, she had gone to the library. The library was empty this time of night. Choosing a cushion from one of the chairs, she settled into a window seat at the far end of the room. It was going to be a long night.

~*~*~*~

Tristan had ridden hard with no concern for direction. Away from people and their sympathies, that was all that mattered. It was dark before he thought to turn and even then, only because his horse stumbled. For his horse's sake, he shouldn't be riding like this.

As he turned for the long walk back through the dark, the thoughts and emotions from which he had run caught him. The grief for his father.

The grief that whatever reconciliation they had begun would never have a chance to finish.

Then, the moment when Jenna had protested the end of their engagement. For a moment, joy had cut through the grief as he had ignorantly assumed that Jenna was as torn up at the prospect of not marrying him as he was. Her comments, though true, had left his heart reeling.

Yet she was the only bright thought in his future. It would not be thoughts of a memorial service that would fill his mind this week. He would think of that when he must. But when he could choose, it would be the wedding preparations that he would fill his thoughts with. There was a bride at the end of this dark tunnel.

~*~*~*~

Jenna woke the next morning with sun on her face. For a moment, she smiled. Then she remembered the previous day. The library window seat where she had fallen asleep suddenly seemed harder.

It didn't seem fair. Losing her own father had been devastating. Now she had found a man who was almost as dear to her as her own father had been and he was gone too. Missing...

With new resolve she sat up and straightened her sleep-rumpled dress as best she could. He was only missing. As long as she didn't know better, she was going to hold out hope. Even if she was the only one in the palace who had any hope left.

Meanwhile, she would be there for Tristan. She would support Tristan as he stepped into his place as king and as he dealt with this loss. She would be there for him, at least, as much as he would let her.

Jenna made it back to her room with no one the wiser that she had spent a tearful night in the library. She half expected Henny to make a big fuss over the fact the king had disappeared. Henny tended to fuss. Jenna sometimes thought that Henny felt that she was doing her longsuffering duty. That perhaps caring for the needs of a commoner turned princess was a questionable honor.

Henny didn't fuss. Instead, she was quieter than normal, caught up in her own thoughts. Jenna was thankful for that. She was especially thankful for the quiet after the dressmaker arrived and there was none.

"Imagine! A wedding during a period of mourning! What was his Highness thinking! It's never been done!"

She clicked her tongue studying Jenna as if she was a seam that had come unraveled. Jenna wasn't sure why she had come, since the dress was done. Nor did she care to risk the dressmaker's wrath by asking. That is, until the dressmaker reached for the dress.

"We'll have to start all over. Maybe something in silver. Still lovely enough to be bridal but passable for mourning..."

"No!"

The dressmaker startled, unable to believe that Jenna was challenging her decision. Her eyebrows rose as Jenna gently took the dress from her hands, cradling it like a baby.

"I'm wearing this dress. A wedding is no place for grief to show."

The dressmaker sputtered, "Well, I…"

Being reminded of her grief made Jenna tear up again but she wiped them away determinedly.

"I thank you for your concern for my appearance. Henny? Will you show her out?"

For once Henny seemed to be in agreement with Jenna. She quickly herded the shell-shocked dressmaker out the door.

~*~*~*~

"No," Tristan said, "I will not delay the wedding."

The council members shifted uneasily.

"But Sire, this is the time to honor your father's memory. At least, put off the wedding until the mourning period is over."

"I can think of no better memorial to my father than to carry out his last wishes. The wedding will take place as planned."

"And the memorial service…"

"Schedule it two days before the wedding."

"The coronation?"

"The day before."

In the face of such certainty, the council crumbled. One man tried one last time, "I don't know if it's wise to have all three events so close together. The work it requires may make it impossible."

"Do it anyway."

A few men were brave enough to send furtive glares his way or mutter under their breath. Others shook their heads. Tristan stared after them in stony silence. He wondered if he had swayed any of them to see it his way.

Chapter 11

Daily walks in the garden became nearly impossible. The castle was in an uproar, preparing for three days of events. The memorial alone was the work of weeks! Amy found enough time to offer condolences to Jenna but didn't dare stay long. With so much work to be done tempers below stairs were running short.

After two days of it, Jenna was ready to retreat to her rooms and stay there but her tutors would have none of it. With the wedding coming up and the added duty of a memorial, Jenna was quizzed unmercifully. Almost every waking hour was filled with lessons.

Tristan was equally busy. The days he had hoped to spend thinking about the wedding were soon filled with the final, legal details surrounding a coronation. When he wasn't busy with that he was being consulted about the memorial and his father's wishes. Still, Jenna was often on his mind. Especially as certain members of the council had not yet given up on postponing or canceling the wedding all together.

Tired of it all, Tristan sat down and composed a note inviting Jenna to an early breakfast on the balcony. Her affirmative response came quickly and eagerly. It was a balm to Tristan's weary spirit.

~*~*~*~

Sunrise came quickly. Jenna, who was used to the country ways of rising early in the morning, was awake. Without disturbing Henny, she dressed, washed her face, and eased out the door.

The balcony where Tristan had asked to meet her for breakfast was the very one that, so early in their acquaintance, had made Jenna's imagination run wild. Even then, him pushing her off the balcony had seemed unlikely. Now, the idea was beyond absurd.

But that moment was what she was thinking of

as she approached the balcony. The early morning light washed Tristan's face in rich color. The sunrise was vivid. Breakfast was already laid out on the table before him.

"Tristan?"

He looked up, "Jenna."

The weight of every worry flew off Tristan's shoulders just because she was here. She had come.

"How are you?" she asked.

"Better," he said, "And you?"

"Better," she said, "Everything seems a little more possible first thing in the morning."

Tristan found he agreed. For a while they spoke of lighter things. The walks in the garden that they had enjoyed. Childhood memories. The beauty of a sunrise. But even when the conversation turned to the memorial, Tristan for the first time found he wasn't buried by the weight of it. Nor was he ashamed to let a tear fall. Jenna took his hand and held on.

Sunrise faded long before either of them were ready. Duty forced Tristan to release her hand and return to his allotted tasks. Jenna lingered on the balcony a little longer. She was marrying a wonderful man.

~*~*~*~

The day of the memorial dawned. Trumpets sounded at sunrise in honor of the king's life. As custom demanded, Henny chose a black dress from Jenna's wardrobe. Though it was a lovely dress, Jenna couldn't like it. It represented too much loss.

Contrary to such a solemn occasion, the day was sunny and cheerful from the start. Birds sang so loud you couldn't help but hear them. Jenna was stubbornly glad for it. A life well lived shouldn't be mourned. If only she could tell her heart that.

By the time of the memorial service, the constant reminders that the king was gone had been too much. As if the loss of him were not enough on its own, every aching moment reminded her of the loss of her own father. When the service began, she had no more strength to hold back the tears.

Tristan, who had escorted her to the service, wrapped his arm around her shoulders. If anyone stared, she was too tired to notice. He, himself, stared straight ahead. Grimly listening.

It was too much. Tristan held fast to what little control he had left, thankful he had Jenna to hold on to. If only they had had more time before the memorial to prepare. To adjust to the idea.

But the memorial had to take place before the coronation. The coronation had to take place before the wedding. And the wedding had to take place when planned. He didn't dare move it even if he had any desire to. Nor did he.

He was thankful when the service was over and the crowds of people offering their condolences had slowed to a trickle. Only then could he excuse himself and escort Jenna from the room. She had regained her composure, but she was still pale.

He guided her to an empty room and a seat by a window. The sunshine was a comfort to him and he hoped it would be to her. From the way she turned her face to it, it was. He didn't dare ask how she was.

"Thank you for being here," he said instead. "If it wasn't for you, I would have been alone."

Realizing that she still held his hand, Jenna gave it a squeeze.

"I'm glad I was here."

They sat in companionable silence for a moment. Tristan near enough that she didn't have to let go of his hand. The sunshine from the window washing over them both. Jenna wished the window were open so she could hear the birds.

"Jenna," Tristan said, "Let me bring your family here for the wedding. They should be with you."

Jenna turned to look at him, surprised. A hope bloomed in her heart.

"Trust me with them," he said, "They'll be safer than you or I."

"I trust you," Jenna said, "Thank you. I would love to have them here that day."

She did trust him. She trusted him with what was most important to her: her family. Now she just had to learn to trust him with one more thing. She had to trust him with her heart.

~*~*~*~

That night Amy brought a tray of food to

Jenna's room. Jenna hadn't ordered it but when Henny opened the door, there was Amy.

"Amy! Come in! Won't you sit down for a moment?"

Henny cast her mistress a scandalized glance then seemed to realize that it would do no good to protest. Amy set the tray down on the table. Then she dropped a little curtsy.

"I'd be honored," Amy answered, casting a glance at Henny.

"Would you like to join us, Henny?" Jenna asked.

Sensing that she was outnumbered, and that Jenna and Amy were both perfectly willing to ignore the fact that Jenna had been elevated to royal status and should not associate with commoners, Henny demurred, opting to return to her room.

With Henny gone, neither Jenna nor Amy felt any need to be anything but themselves. Amy joined Jenna at the small table and Jenna poured the tea.

"How have you been holding up?" Amy asked.

"About like you'd expect," Jenna said. "It's been a hard day. Is that why you're up here?"

"You mean you didn't order a tray?" Amy teased.

That pulled a smile from Jenna.

"Mostly," Amy admitted, "I figured after a day like this you might need a friend."

"How's everyone downstairs taking it?"

"Not much better than you are, I suspect," Amy said. "Even if you never speak to them, when you know how a person likes his toast, you begin to feel like you know them."

They were both silent for a moment before Amy added to her thought.

"And he was a just and kind king; that makes it harder."

"I know," said Jenna.

Amy saw that Jenna was fighting back tears, but fight them back she did.

"Tristan is sending for my family," she said changing the subject, "They'll be here for the wedding."

"Good," said Amy. "That's good."

But the odd tone in which she said it caught Jenna's attention.

"Do you think it's a bad idea? Did I trust him too soon?"

"No..." said Amy. "For all the feathers he's ruffled I've never heard of him actually doing anything underhanded."

When Jenna still didn't look quite reassured, Amy leaned across the table.

"Let me ask you this. Is your mother anything like you?"

"Yes," said Jenna. "Very much so."

"Then she'll be fine," said Amy. "Absolutely, fine."

Chapter 12

The day of the coronation dawned just as bright and clear as the day before. Jenna rose with the sun. Henny still hadn't gotten used to rising so early. Jenna hoped she never would. The few quiet hours of the morning before she had to face anyone had become a treasured part of her day.

This morning she found herself nervous. Not for herself as she would have thought. After all, tomorrow was her wedding day. But tomorrow seemed a long way off. Instead, she was thinking about today. She was nervous for Tristan. Not every man faced the day he would have to accept responsibility for thousands upon thousands of others.

He was going to be a good king. The longer she knew him, the more sure of it she was. The king hadn't needed her to make that true. He had raised a just and intelligent son despite his absences. She wished she could tell him that.

~*~*~*~

Tristan had not slept much the night before. He had not thought to face the responsibility of becoming king for a good many years. Once, before Jenna, he might have rejoiced in it, believing that he could be a better king than his father. It didn't take much to believe that you would be better than a man who had been absent so much of your life.

Now it was a different story. As he had fallen in love with Jenna, he had come to respect his father's wisdom. With that change, and some softening in his father, the wall that had stood between them for so many years had been broken. Now he could see his father had indeed been a kind and just king.

If, for a moment, he could banish thoughts of his father... if he could banish thoughts of receiving the crown, he remembered that tomorrow was his wedding day. One moment he would have a silly grin on face. The next he would remember that he didn't really know what she thought of him. Or how she felt.

And if... when... he could banish both thoughts of Jenna and the waiting crown from his mind, his eyes would close. He would begin to drift off to sleep. Then some memory would come to mind. His father laughing. Jenna, the first night he met her. The anguish he had felt when they had been told that the king wasn't coming back. Tristan had given up sleep long before sunrise.

As tradition dictated, from sunrise until noon the city was silent. Only the birds sang.

Mothers in hushed whispers explained to their children that this is what was done when a prince or princess succeeds the throne following the death of their ruling parent. This was the moment of silence in the king's honor.

Then, as the clocks struck noon, trumpets played. A man, yet a few hours from the city, heard them and quickened his step. In the city, the sound was deafening.

Then a song celebrating the life and events of the king was carried throughout the city and sung by the best of the bards, the town criers, and finally, the people themselves. Due to the rush of the coronation, the most talented songwriters had stayed up half the night perfecting the lyrics. But it was finished. It was perfect.

The more the king was loved by his people, the louder they sang. On this day, before the prince was crowned, the city shook with music. A deaf man could lay his hand on the stones of a wall and feel the rhythm of sound.

Then came silence again as the people waited for the moment when the new king would be crowned. In a small chapel, a select few waited. The chapel was etched in gold that shone in the afternoon sun. Stained glass windows cast colorful shadows across the faces of councilmen and made quilts of light dance on the stone floor.

Jenna was given a seat in the front pew as Tristan's bride-to-be. When she had agreed to be Tristan's bride, this day had seemed far in the future. It seemed impossible to her that they would be sitting here before the king had been given the chance to hold even his first grandchild.

That Tristan would be crowned king before their wedding was almost more than she could think of. When she married Tristan tomorrow... and why had he agreed to go through with it? He wasn't the kind of man who would be intimidated by an uprising of the people. She loved him, could he be fond of her? Sometimes she thought he might be. She thought they were friends. They had come that far, at least... But when she married Tristan, tomorrow, she would be marrying not a prince but a king.

At that moment, he appeared in the doorway of the chapel. His eyes sought hers. For a moment they held. Then, looking to the front of the chapel, Tristan strode forward. He knelt and the ceremony began.

~*~*~*~

The man who had quickened his step at the sound of the trumpets could see the chapel. It was just outside the city on a hilltop. It was part of the royal estate but for generations it had stood apart, a golden beacon against the sky.

The man's clothes hung in rags but in his mind's eye he could see every detail of the inside. The guardsmen who kept the chapel stood sentry. They were ever vigilant today, conscious that not only were they guarding the golden ornaments of the chapel but today they were responsible for the most important of decades. But the man slipped past them with ease.

He was going to be too late. He knew it as he slipped past a second set of guards. He knew it as he flung open the heavy wooden doors. As if in slow motion, he watched the crown settle on his son's head. Unexpectedly, peace settled in him and his heart filled with pride.

Jenna wouldn't have believed that anything could tear her eyes from the sight of Tristan receiving the crown. Then the doors behind her slammed. She turned. There are no words to describe what she felt in that moment. She just couldn't believe that she was right.

And yet she called out automatically. Not the name of the man in the doorway. In that split second before another head could turn, it was a different name she called.

"Tristan!"

He turned. The expression on his face was the same unnamable feeling she felt.

"Father?"

The man in rags had been seized by the guards but the expression on his face was calm and proud. At Tristan's questioning word, the guards pulled back their hands as if burnt. Because they realized that Tristan was right. It was their king who stood before them in rags.

Tristan walked down the aisle seemingly in a trance. Face to face he stood with the father he thought was gone forever. The king reached out and laid a proud hand on his son's arm. When the first words out of his mouth were, "I'm proud of you, son," Tristan broke down.

He threw his arms around him and pulled him in for a hug. The king was every bit as quick to hug him back. They held each other tight for a moment. Then Tristan pulled back.

He pulled the blue velvet cape from around his shoulders. He pulled it over his father's shoulders. Then he removed the crown from his head and set it on his father's.

"Keep it a while longer, Father," Tristan said, "I still have more to learn."

~*~*~*~

It was a confused but jubilant crowd that left the chapel that afternoon. Tristan walked beside his father. Jenna walked beside Tristan. The carriage that had carried the two of them and the chief advisor up the hill carried a family down.

It was evening before they were able to hear the whole story of what happened after the attack. The king had indeed been wounded. Nor did he remember being pulled from the river. The first thing he remembered was waking in a dark shack.

"The fire was glowing in the hearth," he said. "One thing they did have plenty of was wood for their fire. They had precious little else but they pulled me out of the river and nursed me back to health. They were an elderly couple. They had no way to reach help, let alone send word when I revived and was able to tell them who I was."

"Why weren't your people able to find you?" Jenna asked.

"I'm afraid I made it farther downstream than my horse did," the king said ruefully. "It would have saved some time if I could have held on to him."

"How could they have had no way of sending word?" Tristan asked.

The king shook his head, "They were so far out, I don't know how they make it through the winter at their age. I guarantee they'll have all they need this winter, though, and the rest of their lives."

"I'm thankful they were there," Jenna said.

"As am I, Jenna. As am I."

He sent a fond smile to both her and Tristan before he concluded.

"So, since it was the only option, I healed as long as I dared and walked out."

"The doctor tells me your wound isn't healed yet," Tristan said.

"The doctor talks too much," said the king.

~*~*~*~

As they left the king's chambers so he could rest, a courier brought a message to Tristan and Jenna.

"Your guests have arrived, your majesty," he said.

Tristan turned to Jenna with a smile.

"I've had my family reunion for today," he said, "It's your turn."

~*~*~*~

They were waiting in the courtyard as the carriage pulled up. Jenna could see her family through the little windows. The moment they spotted her, the little ones waved and the windows crowded with joyful faces. They were piling out almost before the carriage had stopped.

Her mother was the last one out of the carriage but the first one Jenna threw her arms around. She could feel the arms of her littlest sister wrap around her waist. Her brother, Brandon, had grown. She felt his arm around her shoulders before Alexa pushed her way in. There was laughing and there was crying but eventually Jenna stepped back.

Her siblings suddenly got shy as Tristan laid his hand on the small of their sister's back. This was the crown prince.

"Mama," Jenna said shyly, "this is Tristan."

Her mother saw the look on Tristan's face when Jenna glanced up at him. The worry that had plagued her since her daughter's decision faded away. This was a young man in love.

The king cleared his throat and Jenna blushed.

"And the king, of course, but you know who he is."

"I'm Brandon," said Jenna's brother, meeting Tristan's eye squarely and holding out a hand to shake.

To Jenna's relief, Tristan shook his hand. Then he shook hands with each of her other brothers as well.

"Shall we go inside?" asked the king.

"Yes, please," said Jenna.

And with her youngest sister's hand in her own and her other arm in her mother's, she led her family inside. Falling behind, Tristan and his father watched them.

"Now *that* is a family," Tristan murmured.

"Yes, it is," said his father. "Yes, it is."

Chapter 13

"Tell me again," Stacey, her littlest sister, said, laying her head against Jenna's shoulder.

It was late and her sister wanted to hear about the ball instead of a bedtime story. Jenna had already told her and the rest of her family everything twice. Her brothers had finally been shown to a room of their own sometime after midnight.

Jenna, though she had offered her mother and sisters rooms of their own, had ended up bringing them all back to her own room. Alexa had wasted no time falling asleep. Alana was listening with sleepy eyes to Stacey's begging.

"Hmm," said Jenna, stroking Stacey's hair, "I think twice is enough."

There was no protest. Stacey had fallen asleep. Jenna's mother smiled at her daughters. Alana's eyes finally closed and Jenna and her mother were the only ones left awake.

"I love you," Jenna's mother told her.

"I love you too, Mama."

Jenna eased Stacey down onto a pillow. Then she settled down beside her, laying her head on her arm to better see her mother.

"Mama? I fell in love with him."

"I thought so," her mother said. "He loves you too."

Jenna was quiet for a moment. She thought so too but it seemed like a big thing to assume.

"He hasn't said so," she admitted.

"Give him time. You've come this far, I think you can give him the benefit of the doubt. Are you still sure of this Jenna?"

Jenna smiled with her eyes closed as sleep overtook her.

"I'm sure. I'm so glad I came, Mama," she murmured.

~*~*~*~

When she woke the next morning, the sun

was shining and a breeze was blowing through the open window. Stacey was curled up next to her, a warm pocket against the early morning cool. Alana was on her other side with an arm thrown across her face to block the light.

"Good morning," her mother said.

"Good morning," Jenna said softly.

Tristan didn't want to eat. The ceremony wouldn't take place for hours, yet. He wasn't nervous but he couldn't sit still. Everything was ready. The scene was set, the players in position. Now all they needed was the cue and the wedding would begin.

But before all that, he had promised to meet his father for breakfast. After the experience of losing him, Tristan was eager to spend the time with his father. Besides, it would make the hours pass more quickly.

Jenna smiled as she listened to the squeals. Meeting the dressmaker might not be a fun experience but the gowns that had been brought for her sisters to wear to the wedding had found the right audience.

"Can I have the purple one?" Alexa asked, "Can I?"

Alana couldn't decide so easily.

"Look at this one," she cooed, holding a blue gown up to herself.

Then she traded it for another, "But look at how this one swirls!"

Their brothers had also been given clothes suited to a royal wedding, but Jenna doubted they were having this much fun. Even Stacey and their mother had gotten into the fun, trying on their favorite gowns and dancing around the room. When the dressmaker returned and saw their selections, she merely shook her head.

"All day," she murmured. "It will take all day to alter them."

But Jenna and her sisters were still smiling.

~*~*~*~

Tristan couldn't take it anymore. His rooms were closing in on him. The hallways were brimming with guests arriving for the wedding. Servants carried bags, and grooms stabled the horses. There was no place left in the castle that hadn't been touched by this madness.

"Go," said his father.

"What?" Tristan said.

"Go and saddle your own horse as I taught you and take a ride. It will do you good."

"Yes," said Tristan. "Yes! Thank you!"

He threw his arms around his father and gave him a hug.

"Be back in time to get ready!" His father warned.

"Nothing could keep me away!" Tristan said.

~*~*~*~

Jenna spun in a slow circle. Her wedding gown shimmered around her like moonlight. The lace on the sleeves was a priceless work of art.

Her mother had tears in her eyes. Alana gazed

in wide eyed awe, as if she hadn't been surrounded by beautiful gowns all morning. Jenna felt her own eyes fill with tears and her heart overflow with love for her mother and sisters. She was so glad she was sharing this with them.

"You're a beautiful bride," her mother said. "I'm so proud of you."

~*~*~*~

Tristan felt the wind on his face. The hooves of his horse beat the ground beneath them as if he were riding thunder, flying free. The farther he flew, the more one thought settled in his heart: Jenna. With a wild and joyful cry, he turned his horse for home.

~*~*~*~

Jenna stared into the looking glass. Every hair was in place, held by diamond pins and elaborate twists. If she had thought she looked like a princess at their engagement ball, it was nothing compared to this. The hairdresser smiled.

"You are pleased, yes?"

"It's beautiful," said Jenna. "Thank you."

As the hairdresser left, Jenna thought of one thing that would make this day more special. She reached for paper and ink but Alana snatched them out of her reach.

"Oh, no you don't! One stray drop of ink and we'd have a disaster on our hands. I'll write for you."

~*~*~*~

The message found Tristan as he reached his chamber.

"Dear Tristan," it read, "There is one person here at the castle who has been a dear friend to me since I arrived and that is Amy. Would it be alright with you if I ask her to sit with my family?"

Tristan was startled for a moment. He knew of Jenna's friend among the servants but to invite a servant to attend the wedding would never have occurred to him. His heart softened. This was part of who Jenna was. She was one of the people and she always would be.

~*~*~*~

"Jenna?" asked Brandon in amazement.

It had been agreed the night before that he would walk her down the aisle. He had quickly agreed then, proud to take their father's place, but now he looked nervous.

"You look handsome, little brother," she said.

"I can believe that you're a princess now," he said.

"I'm not until you get me to the end of the aisle."

"Are you ready?"

"Yes," said Jenna. "I'm ready."

~*~*~*~

Tristan's breath caught as the heavy doors opened. The engraved wooden panels and gilded insets were nothing compared to the beauty they revealed. Jenna entered, escorted by her brother. Her dress floated around her. A serene smile lit her face. Her eyes were locked with his.

Yet as her brother handed her off to him, her smile flickered. It wasn't much. Tristan was probably the only one in the room who had noticed. But it was then that he realized that there was something he had to do before they took their vows.

Jenna looked at Tristan, her eyes widening in surprise when he stopped in the middle of the aisle. He cupped a hand around the back of her head and leaned close, his lips brushing her ear.

"Jenna," he whispered, so only she could hear, "I know I should have said this sooner but I want you to know that I love you."

A soft intake of breath and the tears in her eyes were all the answer Tristan needed. He led his bride to the end of the aisle. They exchanged vows and as he leaned down to kiss her, she whispered.

"I love you, too."

Chapter 14

The wedding feast was over. The ball that followed it had come to an end. Daylight was beginning to show on the horizon. Tristan held Jenna
close to him as they walked. As they passed the
balcony he kissed her.

"I have something to show you," he said.

He led Jenna to a wing of the castle she hadn't
been to before. They walked through a luxurious
sitting room and he paused at a door at the far side.
He turned to her.

"I wanted to give you a wedding present that
would mean more to you than pretty things. I
promise you will have plenty of presents of dia-
monds and gold but I..." he hesitated, not sure how
to put into words what he was trying to give her.

Giving up, he gestured at the door, "This is for you."

Stepping past him, Jenna was curious. What was this gift that he was so unsure of? She pulled open the door and looked into the room.

It was like none other in the castle. A heavy wooden table surrounded by chairs sat near a large hearth. The hearth, unlike others in this royal wing, was equipped for cooking and a large shelf to the side held canisters that Jenna suspected held flour and sugar. Bundles of herbs dangled from the ceiling the same way they did in the home she had grown up in.

Unlike the home she had grown up in, a thick rug and cozy seats took up one corner of the room. A rocking chair sat there as well and a shelf with books. Jenna suspected that if she were to read the titles they would be the favorites she had discovered since coming to the castle.

"What is it?" asked Jenna.

Because she didn't know. It looked like home to her.

"It's yours," said Tristan from the doorway to the lavish sitting room. "No one comes beyond this point unless you ask them to. Not the servants, not our families, not me... unless you want them to."

Jenna grabbed his hand and pulled him inside.

"It's ours," she said. "If it's mine, it's yours too. Always."

Smiling down into her eyes, Tristan almost forgot what he meant to say. He remembered just in time.

"When we have children, I want us to be a close family. Those doors there? Those are rooms for our children, so they'll be close by. The other door is our room. I want to have dinners together at that table. I want you to teach our daughters to cook."

"Brandon makes wonderful stew," Jenna commented.

Tristan laughed, "Then you can teach our sons to cook too."

"Thank you," she said. "I love you."

Her eyes were shining. So were Tristan's. Jenna's hand came up to rest on his face.

"I love you," he told her.

Then Tristan kissed his bride.